The TRUTH about Truman School

dori hillestad butler

Albert Whitman & Company
Morton Grove, Illinois

For Linda A., my yoga partner, walking partner, lunch/dinner companion,
movie companion, and all around best friend.
Everyone should have a friend like you!

Also by Dori Hillestad Butler:
Alexandra Hopewell, Labor Coach
Trading Places with Tank Talbott
Tank Talbott's Guide to Girls

Library of Congress Cataloging-in-Publication Data

Butler, Dori Hillestad.
The truth about Truman School / by Dori Hillestad Butler.
p. cm.
Summary: Tired of being told what to write by the school newspaper's advisor, Zebby and her
friend Amr start an underground newspaper online where everyone is free to post anything, but
things spiral out of control when a cyberbully starts using the site to harrass one popular girl.
ISBN 978-0-8075-8095-0 (hardcover)
ISBN 978-0-8075-8096-7 (paperback)
[1. Bullies—Fiction. 2. Gossip—Fiction. 3. Underground newspapers—Fiction.
4. Newspapers—Fiction. 5. Web sites—Fiction. 6. Middle schools—Fiction.
7. Schools—Fiction. 8. Journalism—Fiction.] I. Title.
PZ7.B9759Tru 2008 [Fic]—dc22 2007029977

The design is by Carol Gildar.
Cover photo courtesy of Getty Images.

For more information about Albert Whitman & Company,
visit our web site at www.albertwhitman.com

Can you believe this?

The language arts teachers are making everyone write about what happened for class. I don't mind writing about it; I like writing. I just don't want to write about it for school.

Why should we have to write about something so personal for people who get paid to grade us on our spelling, grammar, sentence structure, and main idea? How are we supposed to write about what happened, or how it affected us, if we're all stressed out about what grade we're going to get?

So I got to thinking . . . if you're like me, and you want to write about it, but you don't want to write about it for school, write two versions: the school version . . . and the truth. Turn the school version in to your language arts teacher (after you check your spelling and grammar, and make sure you have a clear, well-thought-out main idea). Then email the other version to: mystory@truthabouttruman.com.

I'll read through everyone's stories; then I'll cut and paste, change the names, and rearrange the whole thing into one big story . . . the REAL truth about Truman School.

The Truth about Truman
Zebby Bower, Webmaster

 # Zebby:

I am not one of the popular girls. I've never been popular, and I probably will never be popular. But that's fine. I'd much rather have a brain of my own than be popular.

Still, when you think about it, it's pretty amazing that a non-popular person such as myself could launch the hottest website in school. Yes, I am one of the people behind the Truth about Truman.com. The other person is my friend, Amr Nasir. But this isn't a story about me and Amr. It's a story about the website we started and what happened because of it.

I suppose the first thing you want to know is what, or who, is Truman? Truman is our school, Truman Middle School. But because this is the Internet, and for all I know, you could be some freak cyberstalker, I better not say any more about it than that. I'll just tell you it's an average-sized school, in an average-sized town, somewhere in the middle of the U.S. of A. I'm an eighth grader there. Most of the other people you'll meet here are eighth graders at Truman, too.

Believe me, when we started this website, neither Amr nor I had any idea what was going to happen. We started it as sort of a public service.

Really!

You see, before the Truth about Truman came along,

I was the editor-in-chief of the Truman *Bugle*. Don't be too impressed. I only got the job because no one else wanted it. At the end of last year, Mrs. Jonstone asked all the seventh-grade *Bugle* staff members (all *four* of us) who wanted to be editor next year. I, of course, raised my hand because I'm going to be a journalist someday. I'm going to travel the world and write hard-hitting, thought-provoking articles about war, global warming, and all the other big problems facing us today. Being editor of my school newspaper was a good place to start. But Mrs. Jonstone sort of looked past me and said, "Is there anybody else who'd like to be editor next year?" You could tell how badly she wanted somebody, *anybody*, else to raise their hand. It's because of the blue streaks in my hair. Mrs. Jonstone doesn't like kids with blue hair.

But nobody else wanted to be editor, so Mrs. Jonstone was stuck with me.

We butted heads right from the start. First, I wanted to do an article on the new math curriculum and how us kids are just a bunch of guinea pigs because no one really knows whether the new curriculum is going to be any better than the old curriculum until they see whether our test scores go up or down. But Mrs. Jonstone said no to my article. She said, "Students aren't in any position to comment on curriculum."

So then I wanted to do an article on the student council and how it's nothing but a big popularity contest. Once again, Mrs. Jonstone said no because, "Student council isn't about popularity at all. It's about leadership." (Has she actually seen who's on the student council this year? People like Hayley Wood and Reece Weber may be popular, but they don't know anything about leadership.)

Finally, Amr suggested we do a feature article on bullying. I thought this was a great idea because kids like Sara Murphy and Trevor Pearson were always getting hassled at school, and nobody ever did anything about it. This was what you'd call a "timely issue," so I thought sure Mrs. Jonstone would go for it. Besides, I wasn't the one who suggested it; Amr was.

But Mrs. Jonstone still said no. She actually looked Amr in the eye and said, "We don't have a problem with bullying here at Truman, and an article like that would just get the administration all riled up."

I don't know which Truman School Mrs. Jonstone teaches at, but it can't be the one in the average-sized town in the middle of the U.S. of A., because that's the one I go to, and I can tell you we *do* have a bullying problem here. A pretty big one, actually. But you can't argue with someone like Mrs. Jonstone.

The only articles she was willing to run in the *Bugle* were articles on how wonderful our football team was or how fabulous the last band concert was (though she blacked out the part in Ryan Kelley's article where he said the clarinets were flat). Mrs. Jonstone only liked articles that made you go rah, rah, isn't our school great?

Well, guess what? Middle school *isn't* great. And I, for one, was getting pretty tired of pretending it was.

So I quit the *Bugle* in protest.

Our media specialist, Mrs. Conway, tried to talk me out of it. She said, "I know how important the school newspaper is to you, Zebby. Think about this! Don't cut off your nose to spite your face."

But that's exactly why I had to quit the *Bugle*. The school newspaper *was* important to me. It was probably more important to me than it was to any other kid at school. If the *Bugle* couldn't be a true and honest newspaper, then I would start a new newspaper. A newspaper that reported the truth about life at Truman.

My friend Amr was the one who convinced me I was doing the right thing. In fact, he wanted to help.

I only need two words to describe Amr Nasir: Computer Freak. So I wasn't surprised when Amr said, "We should do it online."

I thought publishing our newspaper online was a good idea, too. It would solve the whole how-do-we-distribute-an-underground-newspaper-at-school problem. Our school was pretty strict about what you could hand out at school and what you couldn't. Everything had to be "administration-approved." But if we put our newspaper online, we wouldn't be handing anything out. People would come to us.

Amr and I got started on the website right away. It kind of reminded me of the time when Amr and Lilly and I published the *North Newport News* a few years ago. Of course, that was back before Lilly dumped me and Amr because we were "dragging her down." (That's a whole other story, though it kind of relates to this story.) But Amr and I were older now; we could do a much better newspaper.

We decided to set it up so that anybody could post

an article or a photo. I thought it would be good to let people comment on other people's articles, too. Like a blog. Middle-school kids like blogs!

And they don't like rules. So we only had two for our site:

Rule #1: Whatever you post had to be your original work.

Rule#2: Whatever you post had to be the truth. The truth about our school as you see it.

We decided to call our site The Truth about Truman. We even pooled our money and bought the truthabout-truman.com domain. Then I wrote a short piece for the main page about what this site was all about, and how everyone was welcome to send us material because, unlike the *Bugle,* our newspaper was for everyone, and we weren't going to censor. Anyone could say whatever they wanted. Amr came up with a really cool layout.

Two days later, www.truthabouttruman.com was up and running.

 Amr:

Setting up the site was easy. The hard part was getting people to visit and post on it. I hate to tell you this, but Zebby and I were the bottom feeders of our school. Nobody paid any attention to us.

So, we decided we wouldn't tell anyone the Truth

about Truman was *our* site. We pretended we'd just stumbled onto it, and we walked around school saying stuff like, "Hey, have you seen the truthabouttruman.com? Oh yeah, that is such a cool website. Everyone's talking about it. I wonder who started it?" But that just shows you how not popular we are. The only person who even looked at us when we talked about it was that girl with the bad skin. Sara What's-her-name.

If Zebby and I were bottom feeders at Truman, Sara was even lower than that. I didn't know what the deal was with her, but she never talked. So she wouldn't exactly be spreading the word.

I checked our stat counter every day after school. After three days, we had had a grand total of seven hits. Three were mine. Two were Zebby's. The other two were probably mistakes.

"We need to get other people talking about our site," I told Zebby when we were hanging out at my house. "We need to create a buzz. We need to make people think that the Truth about Truman.com is where everyone goes after school And that people who haven't been on it must not be very cool."

Zebby flipped the blue part of her hair back behind her shoulder. "Yes, because even *we've* been on it!"

"Funny," I said. "But I'm serious. I also think we need to put some stuff up on the site ourselves to get things started. And then we need to add some fake comments to the stuff we put up, so it looks like people are actually reading and commenting already."

Zebby nodded. "Okay," she said.

So we sat down and started writing some articles right then and there. I wrote an article about how five minutes is nowhere near enough time to get from one end of the building to the other, especially if you're coming from the gym. In the time it took me to write that, Zebby wrote two articles.

Her first article was about the new curriculum, which was okay, but her second article really got my attention. "The Truman Middle School Stupid Rules Hall of Fame," I read out loud.

Rule #1 on Zebby's list was: *Students at Truman May Not Use the North Stairs*. Which means if you're coming from music, which is down at the north end of the building on the first floor, and you have math with Mr. Wesack or Mrs. Connor next, you can't go up the stairs that are right next to the music room. You have to go halfway down the hall to the main stairs, go up those stairs, then go all the way back to the end of the hall. Why? Because students aren't allowed to use the north stairs. Nobody knows why.

Rule #6 was: *Students at Truman Are Permitted 10 Bathroom Passes Per Trimester*. I didn't even know about that rule.

"What? We're only allowed to go to the bathroom ten times the whole trimester? What happens if we have to go eleven times?"

Zebby shrugged. "We're out of luck."

"How does anyone know how many bathroom passes we've used during the trimester?" I asked.

Zebby shrugged again. "I didn't make any of these up.

I copied them out of the student handbook."

I turned my attention back to Zebby's notebook. "Hey, this is really good," I said when I got to the part where she wrote, *We at the Truth about Truman do not have an explanation for why any of these rules exist. If you have any ideas (real or made up), please post a comment.* "That's a good way to get people to participate."

"That's what I thought," Zebby said. "Plus I thought it will make people want to come back and see what other people wrote."

"Do you know what else will make people come back?" I asked.

"What?"

"A poll."

"What kind of poll?" Zebby narrowed her eyes at me. "Something with politics?"

"Uh, most kids aren't too into politics," I said.

"Yeah, I know," Zebby said glumly. She read three newspapers every day from cover to cover, so she was always trying to talk politics with someone. "Well, what *are* most kids into?" she asked, chewing on her pen.

"I don't know. Music, sports, video games . . . "

"Should we ask people what's their favorite video game?" Zebby asked.

"No. That's not big enough. We need something bigger."

"Like what?"

"I don't know." But then I thought of something. "How about who's your favorite teacher?" Kids always had opinions on teachers. And our site was supposed to be about our school.

Zebby shook her head. "Everybody would pick Mr. King."

She was probably right. Mr. King was one of the eighth-grade science teachers, and he was awesome! We didn't use a book in his class; instead we mostly did experiments. And they were fun experiments, too. Lots of blowing things up, making noise, getting messy.

"Maybe instead of who's your favorite teacher, we should ask who's your *least* favorite teacher?" Zebby suggested. Which was even better than my idea because people are more likely to tell you something they don't like rather than something they *do* like.

Except, "Won't we get in trouble if we say bad things about teachers?" I asked.

"No," Zebby said. "This is our website, remember? It's not a school website. We can say whatever we want on our website and no one can complain about it."

"Yeah," I agreed after I thought about it a little. "The teachers probably won't even read it anyway." We were having a hard enough time just getting kids to read it.

"Plus some teachers really are bad," Zebby went on. "The Truth about Truman.com can be a safe place to talk about it if you've got a bad teacher. It's another reason people might come to our site."

So I set up the poll. I listed all the teachers by name and then wrote the following headline: "Vote for the absolute worst teacher at Truman." I set it up so it would keep a running total of votes each teacher was getting.

Zebby and I each voted four times to start things off.

I gave my personal development teacher, Mr. Bonham, two votes because he plays favorites, and I gave my language arts teacher, Mrs. Keene, two votes because she just isn't a very good teacher. Zebby gave Mrs. Jonstone four votes, but she agreed with me about Mr. Bonham and Mrs. Keene.

After that we used different logins so we could comment on each others' stories without anyone knowing it was us. And finally, I set up a forum where people could write their bad teacher stories for everyone else to read.

Our site looked way better!

"Now all we need is for someone, anyone, from school to click on our site," I said.

"All we need is one," Zebby agreed. "One person to visit our site, then tell everyone else about it."

"In other words, one of the popular kids," I said.

Zebby nodded.

"How are we going to get one of them to click on our site?" I asked.

A slow smile spread across Zebby's face. "I don't know why I didn't think of this before . . . "

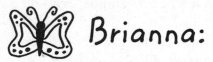 Brianna:

You want to know where I first heard about the Truth about Truman.com? Believe it or not, I read about it in the second floor girls' bathroom. The one way at the end of the hall that no one except us uses. Somebody wrote: "Check out www.truthabouttruman.com" in lipstick on the mirror.

First of all, I don't know why someone would ruin a perfectly good tube of lipstick to write that on the mirror. But it made me wonder what truthabouttruman.com was. So I pulled out my phone and text-messaged Hayley to see if she knew anything about it.

Hayley messaged me right back and said: every1 is talkin bout it. wher hav u been?

Of course, now I wish I had never said anything about that site.

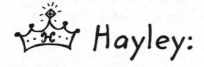

Hayley:

Okay, I never even saw the lipstick message. And if you must know, I had never even heard of the Truth about Truman .com until Brianna told me about it. But I couldn't let her think she knew about something that I didn't! You know how it is.

So when we were in the media center working on our disease projects for science, I waited until Mrs. Conway was busy with some other kids, then I typed in www.truthabouttruman.com and checked it out. I didn't know back then that that weird girl with the blue hair and her nerd friend had started it. I don't think anyone knew, because it looked like a pretty cool site. It looked like the kind of thing someone in our group would've set up. If we actually wanted to set up a website.

"Hey, what are you doing?" Reece asked, peering at my screen. He was at the computer next to mine.

Reece and I used to go out in fifth grade, but I got bored with him and broke up with him after about two months.

"Checking out what's new on the Truth about Truman," I said.

"What's that?" he asked.

"It's a website about our school," I said, like it was no big deal.

Reece checked over his shoulder to make sure Mrs. Conway wasn't looking, then he got on that site, too. And pretty soon Jonathan Nagle, who sat on the other side of Reece, wanted to know what we were doing. Even that freaky girl with the disgusting skin condition stopped to see what we were doing. Talk about a disease project!

That girl really creeps me out. It's not just her skin… she's weird! She doesn't ever say anything. If a teacher calls on her in class, she'll just sit there and stare back at them. She won't even get up and do a math problem on the board. But here she was hanging over my shoulder like it was any of her business what we were looking at.

"Keep moving, Freak," I said. Would you believe she stuck her tongue out at me? Real mature.

"Whose website is this?" Reece asked.

"Don't know and don't care," I said.

There was this list of stupid rules at Truman and you

could write in and guess why the rule existed. Sk8ter-dude, whoever that is, said the reason we can't use the north stairs is because the teachers hang out there and smoke between classes. And Sweetfeet said he or she saw our principal, Mr. Gates, smoking something, and it wasn't a cigarette. I smiled. I didn't have anything to add to that, so I moved on to the section where you could vote for Truman Middle School's Absolute Worst Teacher.

Oh, that was easy! I scrolled down the list and clicked on Mr. Reddy because he took a note Lilly and I were passing last week during this boring movie on the Aztecs. He actually shut the movie off, opened up our note (like it was his business) and read it to the whole class. It was all about Brianna's new shirt and how yellow is so not a good color for her. As her friends, Lilly and I were going to tell her. Just . . . not like that. Not in front of the whole class.

You should have seen the look on Brianna's face when Mr. Reddy started reading. She was so embarrassed. Not to mention mad. So of course that started this huge fight between us.

We made up pretty fast, but still. The whole thing was Mr. Reddy's fault. He's such a totally bad teacher.

As soon as I cast my vote, I emailed all my friends and told them to go to this website and vote for Mr. Reddy for Absolute Worst Teacher.

 # Lilly:

Everyone thinks the whole thing started with Zebby and Amr's stupid website. But for me, it started with an email I got somewhere around the time that website first went up. The subject line read: For Lilly. And it was from somebody who called him or herself milkandhoney.

I had no idea who that was, but I opened the email anyway. There was just one line: *Dear Lilly . . . you are going down!*

My first thought was, huh? Who is this?

My mom wanted to know why I didn't say anything about that email when I first got it. Well, it was just an email. No big deal. I hit delete and didn't think about it again until I got another email.

This one said: *Dear Lilly . . . have you visited truthabouttruman.com yet? If not, you should . . .*

This email bugged me a little more than the first one. I guess because it was the second email from milkand-honey, and I didn't know who that was.

But there was no threat in that second email. Just a question: Have you visited truthabouttruman.com yet?

I hadn't. I'd heard of it. Hayley had sent me an email about it a couple days earlier, but I hadn't gotten around to checking it out yet. After I read that email, though, I got on the Truth about Truman website to see what it was. It looked like an online newspaper about our school. There was an article about the math curriculum that looked kind of boring, so I didn't read it, and another article about how five minutes isn't enough time between classes, a list of Stupid Truman Rules, and a place where you could write about a bad teacher you've had. You could even vote for the worst teacher at Truman. Mr. Reddy was way in the lead. Big surprise. He was always yelling. And if your cell phone went off during his class, he took it away and didn't give it back for like a week!

It didn't say anywhere whose website this was, but something like this had Zebby Bower's name all over it. I should know; I used to be friends with her. We started like five different newspapers together when we were kids. Her, me, and Amr Nasir.

The Truth about Truman.com looked all right. It looked better than the last newspaper Zebby tried to start. At least this time she'd managed to start something that people actually wanted to read. But I couldn't figure out why milkandhoney, whoever that was, wanted me to see it so bad. It was just a computer newspaper.

Then I got the third email.

> *Dear Lilly . . . I know you've seen the Truth about Truman.com by now. You should know there's going to be a special surprise on that website on Friday featuring YOU! Make sure you log on. You won't be sorry. (Or maybe you will? Hahahaha!!!!)*
> *— milkandhoney*

Trevor:

I'm a little surprised everyone's making such a big deal about all this. So, a few people said and did some mean things to Lilly Clarke online. So what? I've put up with way worse things. I've had my head shoved in the toilet; I've been pushed down stairs; and I've had my butt super-glued to a bench in the locker room. I hang out in the media center for half an hour every day after school and shelve books for Mrs. Conway just so I don't have to walk home when everyone else is walking home.

Things got so bad for me last year that I actually went to see Mrs. Horton, the school counselor. Which turned out to be a huge mistake. She wanted me to name names. Yeah, right. Like I would really do that. Was she trying to get me killed?

When I told Mrs. H. to forget it; I wasn't going to tell her who'd been hassling me, she sat back in her chair and made a little steeple out of her two pointer fingers. "Well, then," she said. "Maybe things aren't quite as bad as you're making them out to be."

I didn't know what to say to that, because things were actually quite a bit worse than I was making them out to be. And unless you're the kind of person who avoids going to the bathroom at school and/or has to hang out in the media center after school till everyone else leaves, you have no idea what it's like. So let me tell you: NOBODY LIKES TO ADMIT THEY'RE GETTING POUNDED EVERY SECOND THE TEACHER'S BACK IS TURNED!

So I just said, "Yeah, I guess not," and then I started to get up. At least I'd already missed the first ten minutes of P.E. The other guys would already be in the gym, so the locker room would be safe.

But Mrs. H. pointed to my chair. "Sit back down, Trevor," she said. She seemed surprised that I was ready to leave.

"Let's talk about this some more," she said, acting all concerned. "You're clearly having some sort of issue with your peers."

Clearly.

"Does it have something to do with your mother?"

"No!" I said right away. Because not everything was about my mother.

"Well, then why do you suppose you're having so much trouble with the other kids, Trevor?" she asked, like this was some big mystery she just couldn't figure out.

Well, gee, Mrs. H., I thought. Could it be that this school is full of—never mind. I won't say it. What would be the point? I bet Mrs. H. was popular when she was in school. That was why she said such stupid things sometimes. She just couldn't relate to what kids like me go through sometimes.

Finally, Mrs. H. leaned across her desk like she was about to tell me something that was going to change my life. "You know, Trevor," she said. "Sometimes we do things without even realizing it that sort of . . . set us apart from the other kids. If you could just try a little harder to get along . . . try a little harder to be more like the other kids . . . maybe you'd be happier?"

See what I mean about Mrs. H.?

Basically, she was telling me to just do what every-one else was doing. Be like everyone else, then everything will be fine. Right.

Fat lot of good all that did Lilly Clarke.

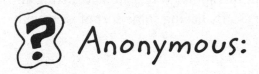 Anonymous:

Write two versions of what happened. That's what Zebby Bower wanted people to do. Write the nice school version for language arts and then write the truth for the website.

Well, guess what? I did that. I wrote two versions. But I have to tell you, the version I turned in to Zebby still isn't the whole truth. I couldn't write the whole truth. Not even for her, because even though she's going to change everyone's name, people from Truman will still be able to figure out who I am, just by what I wrote.

So I decided to write a third version. *This* version.

You won't be able to tell who I am by the things I write in this version. This version is going to be totally anonymous. Which means I can tell you things this time around that I couldn't tell you before. The first thing I want to tell you is: Everyone's making Lilly Clarke out to be this huge victim. Lilly wasn't a victim. She deserved what she got. The second thing I want to tell you is: I've wanted to bring Lilly Clarke down for a long time. I thought I could bring her down by sending her a few emails now and then and scaring her a little.

But then the Truth about Truman site came along. The Truth about Truman made it easy to bring her down.

 ## Lilly:

My boyfriend Reece and I instant-messaged each other almost every day after school. (I LOVED saying that —"my *boyfriend*, Reece!") Technically, I wasn't supposed to be on the computer after school, but after school was the best time to be on the computer because my mom was at work. So I didn't have to worry about her standing over my shoulder and watching what my friends and I were saying to each other.

Almost every time I was on the computer, I had a conversation with Reece going in one window, a conversation with Hayley and Brianna going in a second window, and a conversation with somebody else going in a third window.

Hayley and Brianna were always trying to get me to tell them what Reece and I talked about. Honestly, we never talked about anything very interesting. Most of the time we just did our pre-algebra together. Or we talked about weird things. Like vegetables.

I remember once, Reece tried to convince me that ketchup was a vegetable. I said it was a condiment. We went back and forth for like twenty minutes. Reece was so funny! That's why I liked him. (That, and he was *cute!*)

But I couldn't tell Hayley and Brianna that Reece and I were talking about vegetables. So I just said all mysterious-like, "wouldn't u like to know . . . ☺ ☺ ☺"

"Oooooooooo!" Brianna typed.

I used to think my life was sooooooo great back then. I had good friends, a cute boyfriend, popularity . . . I had everything. But then it all went away. Just like that.

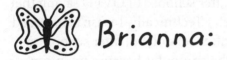 **Brianna:**

Hello? Had no one but me noticed that Lilly was a total *boyfriend stealer*??? Hayley and Reece used to go out in fifth grade! Everyone knew that. Even people who didn't go to Central with us knew that.

Okay. So maybe Lilly didn't exactly steal Reece away from Hayley, but wasn't there like a rule that said you don't go after your friends' ex-boyfriends? You didn't see *me* going after Reece, did you?

But Hayley never complained about Lilly and Reece. She was always all, Oh, aren't they a cute couple? Which

I thought was very mature of her. I'm sure deep down it really bothered her.

Lilly did stuff like that all the time. She was totally selfish. In fact, maybe that was why this whole thing happened? Why people stopped liking Lilly, I mean. And why they posted some of that stuff about her online. If you're the kind of person who goes after your friends' ex-boyfriends, you shouldn't be surprised if people get tired of you.

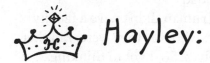 **Hayley:**

So why didn't our group think about doing an underground school newspaper or website thingie? We're the ones who really should be telling everyone about our school because, well, let's be honest . . . we're the ones who run things around here: Me and Brianna and Reece and Jonathan.

Our regular school paper, the *Bugle,* was so lame. Nobody ever read it. People were reading the Truth about Truman, though. They were posting on it, too. You have to admire people who get something going like that. Even if they aren't in our group.

So I got to thinking . . . maybe there was something else our group could get going at Truman. Like . . . a cheerleading squad! We didn't have any cheerleaders at our school. None. Can you believe it?

Last year I asked our principal, Mr. Gates, if we

could start a cheerleading squad, but he said no. He said, "The school doesn't have enough money for another activity."

I said it didn't have to cost money. Lilly, Brianna, and I would cheer at all the football, basketball, and baseball games (wherever there were cute guys!) for free. But Mr. Gates still said no because "it wasn't about paying us to cheer, it was about paying one of the teachers to be our faculty advisor." And the school couldn't do that.

So no cheerleading squad.

But the Truth about Truman didn't have a faculty advisor, either. Those kids, whoever they were, ran that whole thing all by themselves. So, I got to thinking . . . why couldn't Lilly, Brianna, and me start a cheerleading squad all by ourselves? All we had to do was buy some cute outfits and show up and cheer! We didn't need an advisor any more than the people who started that website needed one.

Lilly and Brianna were just as excited as I was when I IMed them my idea later that night. They were all, "yeah, we should totally do it! That would be so great!"

So I said, "Maybe that website—the Truth about Truman, or whatever—would do an article on us? After all, they're an underground newspaper and we're an underground cheerleading squad."

"Maybe," Brianna wrote back. "In fact, maybe they'll even take videos of us cheering and post them on the site?"

"Maybe," I said.

I waited for Lilly to say something, but she didn't. Reece had probably IMed her, so she was probably writing back to him. He was cute, but he was *boring*. And he expected you to drop everything whenever he came online. That's why *I* dropped *him*.

Oh, well. I emailed the Truth about Truman and informed them our school now had our very own underground cheerleading squad and that they (the Truth about Truman people) should come to Friday's game and write an article about us and shoot some video for their website. We could be like their next big feature!

 **Zebby:**

Amr called me to tell me we had some email to answer. It was addressed to the webmaster for the Truth about Truman.

Whoa! "*Some* email?" I asked. "As in 'more than one' email?"

"Yeah."

I slipped on my crocs and hurried down the street. Imagine my disappointment when I saw that one of the emails was from Hayley Wood, and she was blathering on about some brand new *underground cheerleading squad* (give me a break!), and how we should cover it for the Truth about Truman.

I plopped into a chair next to Amr. "Why didn't you tell me one of the emails was from *her*?" I asked.

"What difference does it make who they're from?" Amr asked. "What's important is they're from people who are reading the Truth about Truman."

I just glared at Amr. He knew how I felt about Hayley and Lilly and that whole popular crowd. Didn't he feel the same way? Maybe not. Boys didn't get as caught up in stuff like that as girls did. Which was probably why I preferred to hang out with Amr instead of most of the girls at Truman.

"The thing is," Amr began, "like it or not, if people like Hayley and Lilly and Jonathan and Reece are reading the Truth about Truman, then their friends are probably reading it, too. And if all the popular kids are reading it, then everyone's reading it."

"Yeah, but nobody knows it's *our* website," I said. "If people knew it was ours, do you think anyone would read it? Do you think Hayley would read it if she knew *we* were the ones writing all the stuff on it?"

"I don't know," Amr said. "That's why we have to think about how we're going to respond to her email. We can't cover her cheerleading squad. Not if we're going to stay anonymous." Amr paused. "We do want to stay anonymous, don't we?"

"We definitely want to stay anonymous," I said. "Which means we can't cover the cheerleading squad. Aw, darn." I snapped my fingers.

"No, but we could tell them they can write an article and post it themselves," Amr said. "They can post their own video, too. If they can figure out how to do it."

I made a face. I did not want *cheerleading* stuff

on the Truth about Truman.

"We said this was everyone's newspaper," Amr pointed out. "Doesn't 'everyone' include people like Hayley and her crowd?"

I sighed. I wished it didn't have to. But Amr had a point.

So this is what we wrote to Hayley:

> *Dear Hayley,*
> *The Truth about Truman is everybody's website. That means anyone can post an article or a picture or a video. Feel free to write whatever you want about your cheerleading squad and upload your videos. (Email us back if you don't know how to do it.) I'm sure everyone would love to hear how you started your cheerleading squad and see your video. Good luck!*
> *—Truth about Truman Webmaster*

Amr thought we should say that bit about how everyone would *love* to hear how she started her underground cheerleading squad (as if it were really that hard) and see her video to butter her up (and keep her and her friends reading our site). It about killed me to type those words, but I did. For the good of our site.

"Now who's the other email from?" I asked after I sent our response to Hayley.

"I don't know," Amr replied. "Comicbookhero365. Any idea who that is?"

"Not a clue," I said.

Trevor:

Okay. I'm kind of into comic books. Not just reading them, but drawing them, too. I had this one—well, it was about a math nerd named Nero. Nero was this eighth grader who didn't have any friends. He got picked on and stuff because he was like a human calculator. But then one day he saved this homeless guy's life, and the guy gave Nero super powers, so he went out and he saved the world and stuff. It sounds weird, I know, but it was actually pretty good. I mean, it had a good story. And well, the drawings weren't bad, either.

I just sort of wondered if maybe the people who were doing the Truth about Truman ever thought about having a comic strip on their website? The only thing was, I didn't want them to know who I was because, well . . . let's face it, I wasn't exactly the coolest guy at school. We all know that, right? People would probably laugh if they knew *I* wanted to do a comic strip about an eighth-grade superhero.

Of course, they'd probably laugh no matter what I wrote a comic strip about. Kids at school were always laughing at me. Half the time I didn't even know why.

But everyone likes comics. Even cool kids like comics. Have you ever met anyone who doesn't like comics? It's the most popular section of the newspaper!

So I emailed the Truth about Truman about my

idea. I scanned in a couple frames from Nero to show them I could draw and that I knew how to put a comic strip together. I told them a little about the story, but I also said I could do a whole new comic if they wanted. It didn't have to be Nero. It could be any kind of comic they wanted. It could be a story or a single frame. Color or black and white.

I didn't know what else to say. That was probably good enough.

I signed my email "Comicbookhero365," which was also my email address. I was pretty sure nobody at school knew who that was. Nobody at school even knew I could draw. Then I grabbed my mouse and moved the cursor over to the SEND button. But I couldn't quite bring myself to click on it.

What was I thinking, trying to pass myself off as a comic strip artist? No way would these people who were doing the Truth about Truman, whoever they were, be interested in anything *I* sent them. For a middle-school website, or newspaper, or whatever it was, it was really professional-looking. There were probably ten other people lined up to do comics for them. And all ten of those people were probably way better artists than I was. For sure they were more popular than I was.

But . . . what if no one else had volunteered to do a comic for them? What if they really wanted a comic?

I'd never know if I didn't send the email. So I clicked SEND before I could change my mind.

Forty-five minutes later I had a response:

Dear Comicbookhero365,
  The Truth about Truman is everybody's
website. That means anybody can post an
article, a picture, a video, or a comic strip. We
like your comic a lot, so we think you should
definitely post it. Let us know if you need help.
  —Truth about Truman Webmaster.

Wow! Did I read that right? They *liked* my comic strip? *A lot?* I got goosebumps when I read that! This was one of the best things that had ever happened to me.

I started to imagine this whole big thing where everyone at school would be trying to figure out who comicbookhero365 was. Even the cool kids. And when everyone found out it was me, they'd come up and say stuff like, "Trevor! We had no idea you were so great!"

Before I knew it, *I'd* be the guy everyone wanted to hang out with. I'd get invited to all the parties and girls like Hayley Wood would be all over me. I'd be so busy I wouldn't even have time to be a comic book hero anymore.

 Lilly:

So Hayley decided that if a bunch of kids at Truman could start an underground newspaper/website then she, Brianna, and I should be able to start a cheerleading squad. Well, first of all, I doubted "a bunch of kids" had started that website. Like I said before, I was pretty sure it was just one kid: Zebby. Maybe Amr was in on it, too. Amr was the one who knew all about computers. No way was it a "bunch of kids." Still, I had to agree with Hayley. If Zebby and Amr, of all people, could start an underground newspaper/website, then we should totally be able to start an underground cheerleading squad. I just wasn't sure we could do it by Friday.

We knew there'd be a lot of girls who'd want to do it with us (like Cassie and Kylie and Morgan), but Hayley, Brianna, and I thought it should be just the three of us because, well . . . I don't mean to brag, but *we* were the popular girls.

Hayley also thought that whoever was doing the Truth about Truman could write about us. But if it really was Zebby's website, I knew she'd never do that. She's got a thing against cheerleaders (she's got a thing about a lot of things!), and she sure wouldn't write a story about us for her precious website.

But I was a little surprised when she, or whoever the webmaster of that site was, said *we* could write one. And that we could even upload a video of ourselves. In fact, it made me wonder for a second if the Truth about Truman really *was* Zebby's site.

Brianna thought she could get her stepbrother to record us and send the video in for us.

"So all we need to do now is learn some cheers!" Hayley said.

We also needed to figure out what we were going to wear, and we needed to get some pompoms. I didn't think we had any hope of being ready in time, but no one tells Hayley Wood she can't do something.

So we all stayed after school on Wednesday, and Mrs. Conway helped us find some books on cheerleading. Then we all got on a computer and looked up different cheers on the Internet.

On Thursday we went to Brianna's house and practiced everything we'd learned for like three hours straight. I was surprised how good we were! I think it helped that we'd all taken gymnastics.

Once I was sure we weren't going to fall flat on our faces Friday afternoon, I started getting really excited about this. I always wanted to be a cheerleader, and I always wanted to have a boyfriend who was on the football team (which Reece is!). Back when they were in high school, my mom was a cheerleader and my dad was a football player. I thought it would be so cool if they both came to one of our games. Maybe they'd even remember that was how they got together in the first place.

I know . . . not likely, considering it had been like six months since I'd even seen my dad. And he only lives fifty miles away.

We had so much to do to get ready for that first game that I didn't have time to think about milkandhoney.

Those days right before the game? That was the last time I remember feeling truly happy.

 Zebby:

Amr is my best friend, but he's Muslim, so he can never do anything right after school because he always has to pray for half an hour first. That's why I sometimes stay after school and hang out in the media center with Mrs. Conway. I like talking to Mrs. Conway about books and stuff, and after school is usually the best time to talk to her because the only people who are ever in the media center after school are Trevor Pearson and Sara Murphy.

But one day I went in there after school and Lilly, Hayley, and Brianna were sitting at three of the computers. You could smell their perfume all the way over by the door.

What were *they* doing here? I wondered. Did they even know how to read? (Okay, that wasn't nice.)

I started to turn and walk away, but Mrs. Conway called me back.

"Zebby, come here. That book I told you about last week is in." I knew which book she was talking about—the one about women journalists. I was really anxious to read it, so I held my breath as I walked past those girls and went over to the checkout desk to get it.

"I haven't seen you in a while," Mrs. Conway said as she checked out my book.

"Yeah, I've been busy with school and stuff," I said. I was tempted to tell her about the Truth about Truman School. I wanted to tell her, *See, it was okay that I quit the*

Bugle. *Look at this! Look what Amr and I started. Don't you think this is a way better newspaper than the* Bugle?

But if Amr and I really weren't telling anyone the Truth about Truman was ours, then we couldn't tell Mrs. Conway, either. So I took my book and left.

 *Amr:*

Zebby and I were stoked. People knew about the Truth about Truman.com now. I even saw some seventh graders checking it out at the public library. Every time I saw our site up on some computer somewhere, I thought to myself, that's *our* site. Mine and Zebby's.

"It was just like we said," I told Zebby when she came over late Friday afternoon. "All we needed was one person to find our site."

"All we needed was for the *right* person to find our site!" Zebby corrected. She tossed her sweatshirt onto my bed. "Too bad the right person had to be Hayley Wood."

"Hey, look at it this way," I said. "One reason you don't like people like Hayley and Reece is you think they're users, right?"

"Yeah . . . "

"Well, for once *we're* using *them*," I said. "We're using their popularity to increase the popularity of our site."

Zebby grinned. "That's an interesting way of looking at it."

"So let's see just how popular we really are," I said as I turned on my computer.

Zebby pulled up a chair and I logged in to the domain control panel.

"Look at that!" I cried, pointing at the screen. It was even better than I expected. "We've had a total of four hundred and seventy-two hits since we launched!"

Zebby's eyes about popped out of her head. "That's like half the school."

"Well, only if nobody ever got on more than once," I said. "But still, it's good! It's very good."

Zebby grabbed the mouse. "Let's see what all these people have been doing," she said. "Have they just been reading, or have they been writing comments and posting new articles, too?"

I watched as she logged onto our site.

"They *are* commenting," she cried, surprised. There were two or three comments under most of our articles, and *seven* comments under the Stupid Rules article.

"And look. They're voting, too," I said, pointing to our poll. Mr. Reddy still had the most votes for Absolute Worst Teacher. But one of the math teachers, Mrs. Connor, was giving him a run for his money. (That bugged me a little because I thought Mrs. Connor was a pretty good teacher.) Even Mrs. Horton, our school counselor, had a couple votes for Absolute Worst Teacher.

"We'll have to get some more articles up so people keep coming to our site," Zebby said.

"We?" I groaned.

"Well, maybe other people will start posting articles,

too," Zebby said, scrolling down the site. "Maybe that person who wants to do a comic strip will post the first installment soon."

"And there's a football game today, so maybe this weekend Hayley will post her video."

Zebby wrinkled her nose at that idea, then continued scrolling down the site. "Hey, look!" she cried. "Somebody posted a new poll."

"Really?"

"Uh-oh," Zebby said.

"What?" I said. "What's the matter?"

And then I saw what was the matter.

 Zebby:

Who's the biggest poser at our school?

I read the new question out loud. But it wasn't just a question. If you clicked on the question, you got a picture to go along with it. An old elementary school picture of a girl who was sort of fat when the picture was taken.

Whoever posted this didn't say who it was in the picture. They wanted people to guess who it was. That was the whole point to the poll.

Well, I didn't have to guess. I knew who it was. So did Amr. And so would anyone who had gone to Herbert Hoover Elementary with all of us.

It was Lilly Clarke.

"Wow," Amr said. "Are we really going to leave that

up for everyone to see?"

I turned back to the picture of the unsmiling, fat girl with the greasy hair. And it was like our entire relationship—me, Lilly, and Amr—flashed before my eyes.

I live three houses away from Amr. Lilly lives across the street and down two more houses from Amr. Our houses were all built right around the same time, so we all moved in right around the same time. The summer before kindergarten.

From kindergarten through fifth grade, the three of us did everything together. We walked to and from school together, then spent afternoons running back and forth between Lilly's swing set, Amr's computer, and the old tree house we found in the woods behind my house when we were in first grade. Lilly wasn't fat then. We spent summers at the pool, and winters building snow forts into the hill in Lilly's backyard. We learned how to ride bikes together, we learned how to ice skate together, and we learned how to play T-ball together.

Our parents were friends, too. So on the weekends, our whole families got together. In the summer, our parents would grill hamburgers and then sit out around the fire pit in our backyard while us kids ran around the neighborhood. In the winter, they'd order pizza and play games of . . . whatever it was they played while the three of us hung out in somebody's basement.

Then, when we were in fourth grade, Lilly's parents got divorced.

Lilly and her mom stayed in their house, but things were never the same with our families. The three of us stayed friends (for a while), but our families didn't get together anymore.

Lilly started to gain weight in fourth grade. And I mean lots of weight. She'd always been sort of pudgy before, but in fourth and fifth grade she was F-A-T.

Amr and I never said anything about it, though, because Lilly was our friend. We didn't care what she looked like. Besides, we knew she was going through a hard time.

Then came the summer between fifth and sixth grade. Lilly went away to some camp for most of the summer and when she came back, she was suddenly thin! She was like a totally different person. She got a new haircut and new clothes, and she started taking gymnastics. That was where she met Hayley and Brianna. Hayley and Brianna came from a different elementary school than Amr, Lilly, and I did, but we all ended up at the same middle school in sixth grade.

Most sixth graders still hung out with their elementary school friends. But Lilly started hanging out with her new gymnastics friends. And she made it pretty clear that Amr and I weren't invited. Not that we wanted to be. The only thing those girls ever did was sit around and obsess over their hair, their makeup, and boys.

"Zebby?" Amr elbowed me.

"What?" I blinked.

"What do you think?" Amr asked again. "Can we really leave this up?"

Well . . . we said this was everyone's website. Anyone could post an article. Anyone could comment on an article that's already up. It said all that right on the front page. So how could we not leave it up? Aside from a few votes for worst teacher and a couple of comments on the articles we wrote, this was the first thing someone else—someone other than me or Amr—had posted. We couldn't take it down. Even if it was a little bit mean.

I shrugged. "It's just a picture, right? It isn't any big deal."

"Right," Amr said. "No big deal."

"And it *is* the truth," I pointed out. Lilly really did look like that in fourth and fifth grade. Plus if you asked me, she *was* a poser. Nothing about her was real anymore. Not since she started hanging out with Hayley and Brianna.

So . . . we left the picture up.

 **Brianna:**

My stepbrother was being a total pain. Mark was always a pain, but he was being even more of a pain than usual.

"I don't even go to the high-school football games," he said as shooting sounds came from his computer. "Why would I want to go to a middle-school game?"

"So you can record me and Hayley and Lilly cheering, so we can put it up on this school website."

Mark finally killed whatever he was shooting at on the computer (that, or it killed him?) because the shooting sounds stopped and he turned to face me. "I suppose you'll need me to edit the video and put it up on the website, too?" he said like it was this huge deal. Even though he practically ran the high-school video club single-handedly. He loved video/website stuff.

"Well, if you showed me what to do, I could maybe do it myself," I said in a small voice. Though I hated when Mark showed me anything. He always went through it way too fast and then made me feel stupid when I didn't remember it all. Just because he was really smart and skipped two grades doesn't mean I'm stupid.

"Right. You'd do something by yourself. When have you ever done anything by yourself, Brianna?"

If Hayley wasn't counting on me to get Mark to do this for us, I would have walked away right then and there. Who needs the abuse? But I couldn't go back to Hayley and tell her Mark wouldn't help us.

"Please, Mark," I begged. "I really need you to do this. It's important!"

"Oh, I'm sure it's *very* important," he snorted. But in the end, he agreed to do it. As long as I took his dishwasher duty for the next week.

 Lilly:

It would've been nice if we could've gotten pleated skirts and sweaters like the high-school cheerleaders wore. Not to mention real pompoms. Preferably navy blue and white, like our school colors. But there wasn't time to get any of that, so we decided to wear our Truman T-shirts with dark blue shorts. And then we found some little blue pompoms on sticks at the mall. They were kind of sad looking, but at least we had something to wave around.

When Friday rolled around, we were set!

Hayley, Brianna, and I were so excited all day because we had this huge secret. We hadn't told Reece or any of the other guys that they were going to have cheerleaders on Friday. We hadn't told anyone. I could tell Cassie, Kylie, and Morgan were kind of wondering what was up with us, but we didn't even tell them. The whole thing was supposed to be a surprise!

After school, we went up to our bathroom and got changed. Then we ran back downstairs, bumping into each other and giggling the whole way. We wanted to be down on the field before the football players so we could cheer while they were coming out. That was what the high-school cheerleaders did.

There weren't a lot of people down by the field when we got there, but there usually aren't a lot of people at middle-school games. Just a few kids from school and a few parents who can get off work. They sit on blankets around the field because we don't have any bleachers at Truman.

Hayley, Brianna, and I sort of tiptoed around everyone until we worked our way to the front. Cheerleaders *have* to be in the front! Then we knelt down in the grass and waited for the guys to come out. We kept elbowing each other and smiling because we knew what was about to happen and no one else did.

"Look, here they come," Brianna said, nodding toward the gym door.

Hayley and I both turned. My legs about turned to jelly when I saw Reece was leading the pack.

"It's showtime," Hayley said, nudging me and Brianna. So we all stood up and started waving our pompoms around.

"Here we go, Tigers; here we go!" we said. We started out kind of quiet and unsure, and then Brianna got the giggles. But Hayley glared at her and she knocked it off. We got a lot more serious, and our voices got stronger, and pretty soon everyone was staring at us. The parents, the kids, the players, the coaches, everyone.

There were a couple of kids from my language arts class who, I swear, looked right at me and then started whispering to each other, which made me a little panicky. *Why were they whispering?* Was there something wrong with our outfits? Were we out of step with each other?

Hayley and Brianna just kept right on cheering and waving their pompoms, so I tried to do the same thing, but it was hard when I didn't know what people were thinking. Were they happy to see us or did they think we were being stupid?

But I saw Reece and a few of the other guys sort of smile at us. And then the coolest thing happened. Some of the people who were there to watch the game started cheering along with us! "Here we go, Tigers; here we go!"

When the announcer introduced the players, we all

cheered and turned cartwheels. I was a little worried that the coaches would tell us to stop, but they didn't. So we cheered the whole game.

I think people liked that we were there. At least the people from Truman did. The people from Harding Middle School kind of looked like they wished we'd go away. But they were probably mad that they were losing. And that they didn't have any cheerleaders of their own.

Some seventh grader from the *Bugle* took pictures during the game. He even took one of us. And then when the game was over, he came over to ask us a couple questions so he could write an article about us. Hayley had also written a three-page article about how we started our cheerleading squad for the Truth about Truman. And Brianna's stepbrother was there with his video camera, so we'd have a video to send in, too. It was like the *best* afternoon of my entire life!

Then I went home and everything crashed down around me.

First my mom told me my dad couldn't have me at Thanksgiving after all (big surprise). Something about a business trip or whatever. I wasn't going to let that get me down. After the wonderful afternoon I'd just had, I wanted to stay focused on good things, so I told my mom I had to check my email.

I expected a bunch of emails from people telling me how great me and Hayley and Brianna looked and how awesome it was that Truman now had their own cheerleading squad. But there was only one email in my inbox. It was from milkandhoney.

*Dear Lilly . . . I bet I can take one of the most
popular girls at school and turn her into one of
the most unpopular girls at school. And I bet I
can do it without her, or anyone, figuring out
who I am. Or how I did it. Care to guess which
popular girl I have in mind? By the way, don't
forget to check out the Truth about Truman!*
    Your "friend,"
    milkandhoney

What could possibly be on that website that was
such a big deal? Something about *me*? It had to be if
milkandhoney wanted me to see it so badly.

I opened my browser and typed in www.truthabout-
truman.com.

At first it looked like it was just the same old stuff
that was there yesterday. But then I saw there was a new
poll. Different from the one that was there yesterday.

Who's the biggest poser at our school?

And underneath that header was . . . my old fifth-
grade school picture.

I froze.

I had cut up every single picture we had of me from
when I was in fourth and fifth grade. My mom got really
mad at me when I did it, because now we don't have any
pictures of me from back then. But I didn't care. As far
as I was concerned, if there were no pictures of me from
back then, then maybe I never really looked like that?

But I *did* look like that. This picture was proof.

My entire body started shaking.

It didn't actually say anywhere on that website that

the picture was me, so none of my friends would know it was me. Not at first. I'd never actually come right out and said, "Oh, by the way. I used to be kind of heavy in elementary school."

Anyone who went to Hoover would know it was me, though. So it wouldn't be long before the whole school knew.

I tried to tell myself it didn't matter. My friends wouldn't care. But deep down, I wasn't so sure. I hated to say it, but girls tended to come and go in our group. Like right now, Cassie, Kylie, and Morgan were part of our group, but they wouldn't be around forever. One day they'd say or do something to make Hayley mad and then they'd be out. Just like Leah, Shaowei, and Gabby were.

Would *I* be gone one day, too? Did milkandhoney, whoever that person was, really have the power to turn me into the most unpopular girl in school?

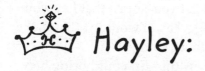 Hayley:

Were we good or were we good? I think more people came up to congratulate *us* than the football players after the game. But I'm not surprised. We really were that good.

As soon as I got home from the game, I uploaded that article I'd written the night before to that Truth about Truman website. I don't know why *I* had to be the one to write it! After all, I was the one who came up with the idea to start a cheerleading squad. I was the one who found our pompoms and decided on our outfits and picked out the cheers. You'd think Lilly or Brianna could have done *something*. But n-o-o-o!

While I was on the site, I looked around. There were a few new bad teacher stories, so I read those. Then I checked out the new poll. It said: Who's the biggest poser at our school? There was a picture of a real lard-butt under it.

Seriously, how does a person let themselves go like that? I didn't get it. I weighed myself every single morning, and if I was up two pounds, I went on a diet. No bread. No cheese. No pasta. Didn't most people do the same thing? Well, people who cared about their appearance, I mean?

Even if you didn't weigh yourself every day like I did, wouldn't you at least notice that your clothes were getting a little tight? Or when you walked by a mirror in a store or something, wouldn't you notice that hey, you kind of looked like Miss Piggy? And wouldn't that make you want to *do something* about yourself?

Honestly, I didn't see how this girl could bring herself to go out in public like that. She had, like, bags of fat hanging off her cheeks and her chin, and she had these beady little mouse eyes and no smile. (Though, really . . . what would someone who looks like that have to smile about?) And it wasn't just that she was fat and ugly and didn't know how to smile. She also had greasy hair. I'm sorry, but there's just no excuse for greasy hair.

I scrolled down to see the results of the poll. Did anyone know who this was? I wondered.

I just about choked. Forty-three people thought it was . . . ME!

Brianna:

Yes! For once, Hayley called *me* instead of Lilly when something was on her mind. It seemed like lately she called Lilly before she called me. Sometimes she even called Lilly *instead* of me. Like Lilly was her best friend now instead of me.

"It's a joke," I told Hayley right away. (Well, as soon as I logged on to www.truthabouttruman.com to see what she was talking about.) "Nobody really thinks that's you."

"Forty-three people do," she whined.

I didn't know what to say. I've known Hayley Wood my whole, entire life, and I can tell you she has never looked anything like that picture. Hayley is like the prettiest girl in our school. She's got a perfect body. Perfect hair. Perfect skin. Seriously, she could be a model. How could anyone think the girl in the picture was Hayley?

"Twenty-seven people think it's Lilly," I pointed out. "It kind of looks like Lilly, don't you think? And nineteen people think it's Shelby Adman. But I don't think it's Shelby—"

"It doesn't matter who it *really* is," Hayley said.

"The point is, forty-three people think it's me!"

"Somebody probably just voted for you because they thought it would be funny, and then everyone else did it, too." It was the only explanation I could come up with.

"But it's *not* funny!" Hayley protested. "Forty-three people at our school think I'm fat. Forty-three people think I'm a poser!"

"Come on," I said. "You're not fat. And you're definitely not a poser. Everyone knows that girl isn't you. That's like so ridiculous it's . . . funny." Even though we'd just established that it's *not* funny.

I waited, but Hayley didn't say anything. Was she buying it? Was I helping at all? I really, really wanted to help.

"I have to go," she said suddenly.

"Wait! Why? What are you going to do?"

"I'm going to call Lilly."

 Lilly:

It had to be Zebby Bower who put that picture of me up on that site. Zebby or Amr. And they probably did it because they're *still* mad that I decided to stop being friends with them in sixth grade. Some people will hold a grudge *forever!*

I could probably just tell the whole school that the Truth about Truman was Zebby and Amr's website and everyone would stop reading it because who cared what *they* had to say about anything? But people would wonder how *I* knew it was their site? I didn't want to have to explain that I used to be friends with them. What would people think?

Besides, even if everyone stopped going on that site, that awful picture was still out there. And I couldn't pretend it wasn't me. Everyone who went to Hoover knew it was me.

What was I going to do?

My cell phone rang while I was trying to figure out what to do. It was Hayley.

"Did you know there's this picture of some lard-butt up on that Truth about Truman website?" Hayley practically yelled at me.

My throat started to close. I couldn't speak. *Did Hayley know the lard-butt was me?*

"It's part of a poll," Hayley went on. "You're supposed to guess who you think it is." Her voice sounded all tight and pinched.

Of course she knew it was me. By now, the whole school probably knew it was me. What could I possibly say to Hayley? She was really, really upset. I could hear it in her voice.

"Lilly," she cried. "Forty-three people think that girl is me!"

Wait—what? "You're kidding," I said.

It didn't sound like she was kidding.

I went to the computer and turned it on. *Come on, come on*, I thought as I waited for it to boot up. *Hurry up!*

When I finally got on that site, I couldn't believe my eyes. Hayley was right; forty-three people thought the girl in that picture was her. And only twenty-seven people thought it was me.

Hayley wasn't upset that I used to be fat; she was upset because people thought *she* used to be fat.

That picture was three years old. Was it possible people had forgotten I used to look like that? If so, there was still time to salvage this. All I had to do was get that picture removed from that website. Which meant . . . I was going to have to talk to Zebby and Amr.

I hadn't spoken to either one of them in close to three years. But I was pretty sure they were the ones who put that picture up. I was even more certain they were the ones who ran that website. So what choice did I have? As soon as I got off the phone with Hayley, I wrote Zebby an email.

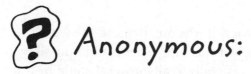 Anonymous:

What? Forty-three people thought the girl in the picture was the most popular girl in school? Were these people blind and stupid? Or just stupid?

I needed to set the record straight.

 Zebby:

"i just got an email from Lilly," I instant-messaged
Amr on Saturday. "did u get one, 2?"

"no. what duz it say?"

I picked up the phone and called Amr so I could
read it to him. "It says, 'I know you and Amr are the
people who started the Truth about Truman.com, but I
bet no one else does. I also know that you guys are the
ones who put that picture of me up on your site. I want
you to take it down. If you take it down before anyone
guesses it's me, then I won't tell anyone that it's just you
guys doing that site.' Can you believe that? 'Just you guys,'
like we're nobodies or something."

"We *are* nobodies," Amr pointed out.

"Yeah, well…" I paced back and forth in my room.
"She didn't need to say so." It just reminded me we
weren't all friends anymore. Sometimes it was hard to
believe we ever were.

"Did she say anything else?" Amr asked.

"No. That was it." Wasn't that enough?

"Are you going to write back?"

"Yes, but I'm still figuring out what I'm going to say."
So far, I was thinking something along the lines of, *First
of all, we don't care that you know it's us. Second of all,
what makes you so sure we're the ones who posted that
picture of you? Anybody who went to Hoover could have
taken it out of our fifth-grade memory book. I'm sure we're*

51

not the only people you've ticked off. And third of all, we're NOT taking it down! Where do you get off talking to us like that? You're no better than we are. In fact, you—

"Uh . . . it probably doesn't matter what you say," Amr said all of a sudden. I could hear him typing in the background. "It looks like we're too late."

"What do you mean we're too late?"

"Go to the site."

I sat back down at my desk. Cradling the phone between my shoulder and my ear, I typed in www.truthabouttruman.com. It was kind of slow loading this time. Was that because there were a lot of people trying to load it right now?

When the page finally came up, I clicked on the Who's-the-biggest-poser-in-our-school link. If I thought the main page was slow to load, this page was even slower.

"Is it loading slow for you, too?" I asked Amr.

"Yeah. You'll see why in a minute."

Finally, Lilly's picture came up.

But it looked different. Someone had gone in and edited it! They made her eyes bigger, and drew horns on her head, a mustache under her nose, a beard on her chin, and two big teeth hanging down from her closed mouth. There was a box with an arrow pointing to the teeth that said click here. So I did, and a little speech bubble popped out of Lilly's mouth. It said, "Oink! Oink! I am Lilly Clarke."

Trevor:

Since the people at the Truth about Truman said they liked my story about Nero, I decided to go ahead and post the first segment of my comic (six frames) on the site. A lot happens in those first six frames. Nero goes from math nerd to superhero, and then he's warned to use his powers for good and not evil. That seemed like a good place to break because if people thought it was stupid, I wouldn't ever have to post anything else. But I could post more if people liked it.

So I uploaded the comic to the Truth about Truman that weekend. I tried not to check the site too often for comments, but it was hard not to. I really wanted to know what people thought.

I was actually thinking about entering the full comic book in the Galaxy Publishers' teen comic-book writers contest. If I could get it done on time. And *if* people who saw it on the Truth about Truman liked it. If nobody liked it, well, then maybe I wouldn't bother.

So far, no one was saying anything. *Why weren't they saying anything?*

There sure were a lot of comments about that old picture of Lilly Clarke, though. Every time I checked the site that weekend, there were at least two new comments about how fat Lilly used to be, or what an improvement the horns and mustache were, or how shocked someone was to find out that was *Lilly!*

I knew Lilly when she used to look like that. We weren't friends, but we went to the same elementary school. I remember when we were in fourth grade, Justin Sawyer was making fun of my sponge painting in art. Lilly told him to stop, but he wouldn't, so she "accidentally" spilled the black paint in his lap.

She was a whole different person now. Always trying to impress the popular kids. The worst thing was last year when she told me I was so ugly that my mom would probably keel over and die of embarrassment for giving birth to me. Which wouldn't have been such a big deal if my mom didn't *really* "keel over and die" two days after that. I know it was just a coincidence. Lilly didn't make it happen or anything. My mom had a blood clot in her brain and she died. Just like that.

Lilly went out of her way to avoid me the whole rest of the year. We had two classes together, science and language arts. But somehow she managed to get her schedule changed in the middle of the trimester so we weren't in those classes together anymore. And now, anytime she sees me in the hall, she says to her friends, "Oh, there's Trevor. Ew, he stinks. Let's go this way." And then they all turn around and walk the other way.

The thing is, people like Lilly and Reece and the other popular kids could choose to use their powers for good. Like Nero. Everyone listens to them. So they could just say hey, we're not going to pick on people anymore. And the whole school would follow their lead. But they don't do that. Instead they use their powers for evil.

 Lilly:

I don't know if I was just paranoid or what. But I sort of got the impression my friends were avoiding me after that picture went up. First, Hayley's mom called my mom and asked if I could get to school on my own on Monday because Hayley had to go in early to work on a science project. Maybe she really did have to work on a science project, but why didn't she mention it earlier?

And what about Brianna? She and I were in the same science class, so I knew she didn't have any special science project. She and I could have made carpool arrangements. But I didn't call her, and she didn't call me. And I ended up getting a ride to school from my mom instead of Hayley's mom.

Then when I got to school, there wasn't anybody waiting at the rock. I knew Hayley wouldn't be there, but I expected Brianna, Cassie, Kylie, and Morgan to be there. Our group always met at the rock before school, and then we walked in together when the bell rang.

But that Monday I had to walk in all by myself.

The whole way to my locker it felt like everyone was staring at me. I even saw a couple of girls from my history class whispering behind their hands when I walked past.

"You know, that Truth about Truman website is Zebby Bower's and Amr Nasir's," I said to the whisperers.

They stopped whispering and just stared blankly at me.

"The girl with the blue hair and her dork friend?" I said.

Still no reaction. Which only proved what big losers Zebby and Amr were. No one even knew who they were!

"You shouldn't believe everything you see on the Internet," I said. Then I walked away.

When I got to my locker, I hung up my jacket and gathered all my stuff for my morning classes. Then I hurried to our bathroom (the one that Hayley claimed as ours at the beginning of the year).

No one was there, either!

Well, the door to the middle stall was closed, so obviously *someone* was in there. But just one person? Where was everyone else?

Normally, this bathroom was hopping in the morning. Girls whose parents didn't let them wear makeup crowded in close to the mirror so they could quick get their makeup on, while the rest of us complimented each other on our outfits and put the finishing touches on our hair. Other people traded homework or talked about who was going out with who or whatever.

"Hey," I said to whoever was in the bathroom, but they didn't answer. So I went over to the mirror to check my makeup and fix my hair.

The toilet flushed and I watched in the mirror to see who came out of that stall. I gasped. It was that weird girl who never talks!

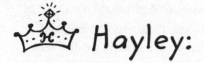 Hayley:

Despite what everyone was saying, we did not dump Lilly when we found out she used to be fat. We are not that shallow! We thought it was really amazing that she lost a ton of weight and was popular now.

But I have to admit, I was a little bit traumatized by the fact that people thought it was *me* in that picture. (Can you blame me?) So . . . maybe we didn't exactly defend Lilly when people started saying bad stuff about her. And maybe we kind of avoided her a little bit at first while we waited to see how people acted around her at school.

But we didn't *dump* her. Not right away.

 Trevor:

What can I say? People at our school suck.

Mrs. Holbrook was late to social studies, so while everyone else was goofing around, I worked on my comic book (just in case I decided to enter it in that teen comic book-writing contest). I already had the whole thing sketched out in pencil (twenty-four pages!), so I was inking over the pencil marks. I wasn't paying any attention to what everyone else was doing.

All of a sudden Brianna Brinkman reached across

the aisle and snatched the booklet right out from under me. "Look everyone," she teased, holding the booklet out of my reach. "Trevor's drawing a comic book!" She flipped the pages and laughed out loud. "Hey, it looks like *Trevor's* the one who drew that comic on the Truth about Truman! You know, the one about the superhero? I've got the whole thing right here."

I could feel my face growing warm. "Give it back!" I cried.

I tried to grab my book back, but then Reece called out, "Let me see it!" So Brianna tossed it over to him. Then several other kids grabbed it.

"Oops," Taylor Bryson said as the cover tore off in his hand.

NO! I didn't have another copy yet. I hopped over the chair in the next aisle and lunged for the book, not sure whether to go for the book or the cover. But it didn't matter since I couldn't get either one. Kids just kept laughing and passing the pages around.

I did manage to grab page seven, which had landed on the floor. The top corner was crumpled and it had a big dusty footprint across it.

"Hey, Trevor! Is this supposed to be *you*?" Reece sneered, holding up a page of my book. "Do you think you're a big superhero?"

"Just give it back," I said, my voice cracking.

This went on until Mrs. Holbrook finally came in to start class. "What's going on here?" she demanded, hands on her hips.

Everyone scrambled for their seats, leaving what was

left of my comic book spread out on the floor. Sara Murphy got up and helped me gather up the torn and crumpled pages. Most people think she's even weirder than I am, but they only think that because she has eczema and she doesn't talk. Still, she was only one who bothered to help me gather up my book.

"Thanks," I mumbled as she handed me a stack of pages. But the pages were all out of order, and I was missing the cover and half of page three. So much for entering it in the Galaxy Publisher's contest.

 ## Lilly:

I paced back and forth outside the noisy cafeteria. Dishes clattered and people were talking and laughing. I could see my friends crowded around our usual table over by the windows. Hayley, Brianna, Cassie, Kylie, and Morgan. The popular girls. There was an open seat between Hayley and Brianna. I could just walk over there and sit down like it was any other day, but . . . what if they all got up and left the minute I did?

They wouldn't do that, I told myself. *Those girls are your friends. Don't be afraid to go over there. You belong there.*

Or I could go sit with Reece and his friends. This wasn't boyfriend day, though. We didn't normally eat with the boys unless we'd all decided it ahead of time.

The boys would probably think it was weird if I showed up at their table by myself. Plus, they could have seen that picture of me, too. And they might make a bigger deal of it than the girls. Boys weren't always the most mature people in the world.

In the end, I decided it was better to take a chance with the girls. So I forced myself to walk over there. "Hi," I said, forcing a smile. I plopped my books and my lunch bag down on the table.

Cassie and Kylie looked up at me, but neither one said a word. Morgan kept her head bent over her sandwich. Hayley was the only one who spoke to me.

"Hey, Lilly." She smiled back, pulled out my chair and patted the seat. "We were wondering where you were."

"You were?" Why was Hayley acting all friendly to me when no one else was even looking at me?

"Sorry I didn't wait for you by the rock this morning, Lilly," Brianna said as she stirred her yogurt. "I had to put lunch money in my account."

"And I had to return a library book," Cassie said.

"Me, too," Kylie piped in.

I just kept trying to act normal. "That's okay," I said like I hadn't even noticed they weren't at the rock. I unzipped my lunch bag and took out my turkey sandwich.

"We did wait for you in the bathroom, though," Hayley said.

What?

"N-no, you didn't," I said. "I was in the bathroom. I was there until the bell rang. You guys never came in."

You left me in there alone with Sara Freakazoid Murphy!

They all looked confused. "Yes, we did," Cassie insisted.

"We were there until the bell rang, too," Kylie said.

I didn't know what to say. They *weren't* there. I knew they weren't. Why would they lie about it to my face?

"Uh-oh," Brianna said, slapping the side of her head. "Didn't you get the email?"

I looked at her. "What email?"

"I don't really like having our bathroom so far away from everything," Hayley said with a shrug. "So I decided we should claim the one by the front stairs instead. I emailed everybody last night."

Hayley moved our bathroom? Just like that?

"That creepy Sara Murphy was in there putting gunk on her arms," Cassie said, wrinkling her nose. "At first I didn't think she was going to leave."

"Yeah, we all walked in and Hayley goes, 'This is *our* bathroom now. From now on, your bathroom is the one on the second floor at the end of the hall,'" Morgan said, imitating Hayley's voice perfectly. "But she just ignored Hayley and kept putting that stuff on her arms."

"So we all sort of moved in closer to her," Brianna said. "After all, there were five of us and one of her—"

"Yeah, and then she all of a sudden spun around and raised her arms like she was going to touch us!" Hayley said. "So we all jumped back because she had that *stuff* all over her hands."

"Then, you know what she did?" Brianna asked me. "She started laughing!"

"She has the most bizarre laugh you've ever heard in your life," Kylie said.

And everyone else nodded and laughed.

"I didn't get any email," I said.

"Really?" Hayley said. She shrugged. "I wonder why not?"

 Amr:

I really hate it when people ask me what religion I am. Most of the time they already know when they ask; I'm Muslim. They just like to hear me say it so they can act all shocked. Like no Muslims live in the United States.

FYI . . . I was born in the United States. My parents come from Jordan and we are Muslim, but I'm as American as anyone else at school. I just don't celebrate Christmas; I pray five times a day; I fast for Ramadan, and I don't eat pork or drink alcohol.

I also can't date or go to dances. Sometimes kids give me a hard time about that. Like back in sixth grade Lilly told me she wanted to be my girlfriend and go to the fall dance with me. She knew I wasn't allowed to go to the dance, so I couldn't figure out why she asked me. And I was trying to figure out a nice way to tell her I couldn't go since it seemed like she really wanted to go with me.

Then I found out the reason she asked was because her new friends thought it would be funny if she *pretended* she wanted to be my girlfriend. The whole point was to make me look stupid and make fun of me because of my religion.

After they admitted it was all just a big joke, Lilly said to me, "I suppose I'm on your terrorist list now." I gaped at her. "What?" I said. I couldn't believe she'd say something like that to me. Lilly was my friend. Or she used to be. She knew how much a comment like that hurt.

Then Brianna said, "Are you going to blow us all up when we grow up, Amr?"

And then they all laughed—her, Lilly, and Hayley.

Kids say things like that to Muslim kids all the time. I know people at Saturday School who don't want any of their school friends to know they're Muslim. One girl I know wears her hijab to mosque, but not to school. It's like she's ashamed of who she is.

I'm not ashamed of my religion. If any of my friends have a problem with me being Muslim, then they're not really my friends.

I guess that was how I knew for sure that I didn't just "have a fight" with Lilly back in sixth grade. Lilly stopped being my friend.

Some things you just don't joke about. Lilly didn't get that back in sixth grade, but maybe she was starting to get it now? With me, you don't joke about being Muslim or being a terrorist; with Lilly you don't joke about her being fat.

 # Lilly:

We never talked about that picture. I knew all my
friends saw it. I knew they all knew it was me. But we
never actually talked about the fact that I used to look
like that. We never talked about the fact someone had
gotten hold of that picture and put it online. And we
never talked about the fact that people were saying some
not very nice things about me on that website.

I got a few anonymous emails. Not just milkandhoney;
other people, too. They said things like, "Wow, you used
to be really fat!" Or, "Be careful, Lilly. It looks like you're
gaining a few pounds . . . " Or, "If you start getting too fat,
your friends will drop you." But for the most part, people
were treating me pretty normal to my face. I mean, at
first it was just the one day that Hayley's mom didn't give
me a ride to school. We rode together every day after that.
Hayley, Brianna, and I either went to the media center to
look up new cheers after school or we went to the gym
to practice our cheers. And Reece still called or IMed me
every night. So on the outside, everything seemed normal.

But something still felt off to me. Like maybe things
weren't really what they seemed. And I couldn't help but
wonder if it was some of my friends who had sent those
anonymous emails. But maybe that was just me being
paranoid again.

People think that if you're popular, you've got it made.

But that's not true. You have to work at being popular. You have to wear the right clothes and hang with the right people and do the right things . . . It's *hard* because people are always watching and waiting for you to screw up.

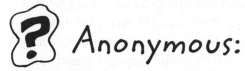 **Anonymous:**

Spreading that picture around was just step one in my plan. I wanted everyone to know that Lilly was not always the person she appears to be now. She wasn't always so special.

When things started to die down, I put phase two of my *Bring Lilly Down!* plan into action.

 **Zebby:**

Now that the Truth about Truman had readers, I worked my butt off to keep them. I cranked out new articles as fast as I could. I archived anything that was a week old and wasn't getting comments, like the article I did on the new math curriculum. I couldn't believe it. The new math curriculum affects every student at Truman, but not one person had anything to say about it.

Lots of people commented on Amr's article about the short passing time between classes, though. And 103 people had commented on Lilly's picture. It's just no one was commenting on the stuff that really mattered.

Well, what could you expect from middle-school kids? I hoped the new stuff I was putting up would interest them a little more. I wrote about the quiz bowl taking second in the state, the drama club's auditions for *Wizard of Oz,* and I listed new books that the media center just got, you know, stuff you'd see in a regular school paper.

Then there was the day-old cupcake incident. Believe it or not, our school sold "day-old" cupcakes, and some of those cupcakes turned out to be moldy! But you couldn't tell they were moldy until you took the wrapper off. Amr about lost his whole lunch when he noticed the mold on his cupcake.

"Yuck," I said. "I'm glad I didn't buy one."

I looked around to see how many other kids had bought them. Sara Murphy had. Most people won't let her sit at their table, so she usually sat at the other end of our table. Amr warned her. "You better not eat that. Mine was moldy."

But she acted like she didn't even hear Amr. We both watched as she slowly unwrapped her cupcake and shoved the whole thing in her mouth without even checking to see if it was moldy. It was like she was taunting us or something. I don't know . . . she could be a little weird.

Anyway, the whole thing gave me an idea for a big feature story—School Food: Is it Safe???

We wrapped up Amr's moldy cupcake and brought it home so we could take a picture of it for the Truth about Truman. "Day-old" cupcakes indeed! More like month-old, I'm guessing.

Personally, I didn't think the school should even be allowed to sell stuff that wasn't fresh. McDonalds throws out hamburgers that have been sitting out for more than ten minutes. The health department says they have to. Doesn't the health department have rules about what schools can serve, too? I decided to call the health department and find out.

Guess what they said? Schools aren't supposed to sell day-old food at all! And guess what else? The lady I talked to at the health department said they would schedule a "surprise" visit to Truman to make sure they were up to code on everything.

I didn't know whether any teachers read the Truth about Truman, but just in case they did, I decided not to write about the health department's surprise visit. I still had enough material to write a really good article. This was going to be the lead story on the site.

Or so I thought.

The day my article about school food went up on the site, something else appeared that got people talking even more than my article and the picture of Amr's moldy cupcake:

Secret! Secret! Who's Got a Secret!

What did you all think of that picture of Lilly Clarke? She used to be a real porker, didn't she? Well, guess what? She's got an even bigger secret than that. Log in to this site again tomorrow to find out what it is.

—milkandhoney

 ## Trevor:

Milkandhoney? Who's milkandhoney? It was like that was all anyone talked about at school. Some people thought it was Zebby Bower because she and Lilly used to be friends and now they weren't. Plus she was the one who started the Truth about Truman website. But other people thought it was somebody in the popular group. Somebody who wanted to nudge Lilly out.

Nobody asked my opinion on the whole thing. Which was fine. If I'd named somebody, no matter who it was, I probably would've gotten my head shoved in a toilet. And if I didn't name a name, I probably still would've gotten my head shoved in a toilet. A guy like me can't ever win.

 ## Lilly:

Enough was enough. I was not going to let Zebby and Amr ruin everything I'd worked so hard for the past two years. Zebby ignored the email I sent her, so this time I picked up the phone and called her. I hated that I still had her phone number memorized.

"I want you to stop," I said right away when she picked up. I saw no reason to make small talk.

Pause. "Who is this?" Zebby asked.

I couldn't believe she didn't recognize my voice. Or check her Caller ID. "It's Lilly!"

"Oh," Zebby said coolly. I could tell by the way her voice changed that she really didn't know who I was until I told her. "What do you want?"

"I just told you what I want! I want you to stop. Stop sending me emails, stop posting stuff about me on your stupid website, stop everything!"

Zebby paused again. "I don't know what you're talking about."

I sighed. Did I have to spell it out? "Milkandhoney?" I said. Duh!

"What about it?"

"I know you're milkandhoney," I said, daring her to deny it. "In fact, I'll bet it's you and Amr together."

Zebby let out a short laugh. "It is not!"

"Right."

"It's not! I don't even know any 'secrets' about you anymore," Zebby said. "In case you hadn't noticed, we haven't exactly been hanging out much lately."

Thank God for that. "Well, maybe it's something from back when we were hanging out."

"Like what?" Zebby asked. "I thought your big secret was that you used to be . . . well, heavier than you are now. And not very popular. But everyone already knows that now."

"Thanks to you! It's your website, so it has to be you spreading all that stuff around. You or Amr."

"How do you know it's our website?" Zebby asked.

I rolled my eyes. "Please. Everyone knows."

"Really?" Zebby actually sounded happy about that.

"Don't sound so excited," I said. "I'm not going to let you ruin my life."

"Ruin your life?" Zebby let out a short laugh. "I have news for you, Lilly. I don't care enough about you anymore to bother ruining your life!"

I felt a little chill when she said that. What if she was telling the truth? If Zebby wasn't milkandhoney, then I had no idea who was. Or what that person thought they knew about me.

 **Zebby:**

A lot of people figured out that Amr and I started the Truth about Truman, but they didn't care! They read it anyway. A couple kids even came up to me in the hall and said, "Great site, Zebby!" I don't think I got this much attention when I put blue streaks in my hair. That just goes to show you there was a real need for a newspaper that represents our whole school. Even if a few people were using it for purposes other than what we originally intended.

 **Lilly:**

Zebby and Amr probably think I'm this horrible person who dropped them in sixth grade just so I could join the popular crowd.

It wasn't like that. Well, maybe it was sort of, but it wasn't anywhere near as cold as that. We grew apart. That's it. That's all that happened. My parents "grew apart." According to my mom, that's why they got divorced. Well, sometimes friends grow apart, too. Especially in middle school.

Zebby and Amr, they just don't care about a lot of the same stuff I care about. There was this time in sixth grade when we were all walking home from the mall together, and they started singing! Right out in public! And it wasn't even a real song; it was just some random, bizarre-O thing. The point is, I told them to stop because people were looking at us, but they wouldn't stop. In fact, they locked arms and started doing it *louder*. They even started skipping. It was totally immature. Not to mention embarrassing.

No matter what we were doing, whenever I ever said to them, "You guys, people are looking at us!" their response was always, "So?"

They didn't care. They never cared what anyone thought of them. It was like they were still in elementary school. They just wanted to run around, sing stupid songs, and hang out in the tree house. I was past all that.

And, well . . . when I lost all that weight right before sixth grade, the popular girls welcomed me into their group.

It wasn't that I dropped Zebby and Amr for the popular crowd. Once we got to middle school, I found a crowd that suited me better than they did. Did that really make me such a terrible person?

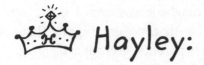 # Hayley:

A lot of people probably don't realize this, but it's a lot of WORK being popular! And if you're like the *most* popular girl in the popular group, it's even more work because you have to figure out what's in and what's out and who's in and who's out. The whole school depends on you to tell them stuff like that.

Sometimes I like to sort of push the envelope, if you know what I mean. Like once I told people that these really tacky shirts from Target were in. Hello! They were from *Target!*

But it didn't matter. The very next day like five girls came to school in those ugly shirts.

It makes me wonder sometimes . . . how far could I go? What kinds of things would people like Brianna or Cassie or Kylie do for no other reason than I told them to?

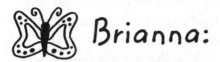 # Brianna:

I don't mean to sound whiny or anything, but no one ever listens to me. If people had listened to me back in sixth grade, we never would've started hanging out with Lilly. I never understood what Hayley or anyone else saw in her. She wasn't all that pretty. She didn't have a great personality. She didn't even live in a very nice house.

So why did Hayley let her start hanging with us back in sixth grade?

We first met Lilly at gymnastics the summer before sixth grade. She was new at gymnastics that year, and I remember she was totally scared of the uneven bars. Isn't that weird? I mean, why would you even sign up for gymnastics if you're scared of the uneven bars?

But she was. And I think she was scared of the balance beam and the vault, too. She only liked the floor exercise. We didn't pay much attention to her at gymnastics since we didn't know her. When we saw her at Truman in the fall, we were like, "Hey, we know you," but it wasn't any big deal. We still didn't start hanging out with her. That didn't happen until I had my appendix out.

I'm not entirely sure how it happened since I wasn't there. I was in the hospital. But Hayley said there was an uneven number in gymnastics that day and somehow she and Lilly ended up spotting each other. Then they ended up sitting together at lunch at school. I have no idea how *that* happened. And before I was even up and around after my operation, Lilly had wormed her way into our group.

I didn't get it. Couldn't Hayley see that Lilly just wasn't one of us?

But Hayley seemed to think she was exactly like us. *Better* than us even.

"Look how everyone turns and watches her when she walks down the hall," Hayley said. "She must've been really popular at her old school. So if we hang with her, we'll be popular, too. You want to be popular, don't you, Brianna?"

Of course I wanted to be popular. But I wondered if Lilly was really as popular as Hayley thought she was. I mean, she didn't dress like a popular girl. Not back then. But Hayley was right about people in the halls gawking at her. Everyone always turned and looked when she walked by. Like I said, I didn't get it. But, whatever. We started hanging with her. And by Christmas, the three of us were the girls everyone wanted to be friends with. We were the popular girls.

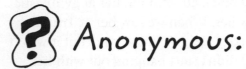 Anonymous:

Have you ever noticed that people say and do things online that they would never do in real life? It's true. For instance, I would never go up to Lilly and say, "Wow, you used to be really fat," but I don't have any problem saying that to her online.

It's different online. You can say or do whatever you want online because no one has to know it's you saying or doing those things. And you don't actually have to face the person you're being mean to.

 Lilly:

The next morning, as soon as my mom got in the shower, I hurried into the living room and turned on our computer. My mom didn't like me getting on the computer before school, but I had to see if milkandhoney had posted my "secret" yet. My fingers were shaking so bad I could hardly type www.truthabouttruman.com.

When the site came up, I saw huge block letters at the top of the screen:

LILLY CLARKE IS A LEZBO!

What?!

There were three sentences in smaller letters below the headline. *Don't believe me? Click* here *to read Lilly's blog. Find out who she's in love with.*

I gasped. I didn't have a blog! And everyone already knew who I was "in love" with—Reece!

I was scared to click on that link, scared to see what I might find there. But not clicking on it was even scarier. I had to know what was on there before I went to school. So I clicked . . . and I found myself on a website that was all done up in purple (which happened to be my favorite color). It had lots of pictures and animations. There was a picture of me in the upper right hand corner (my normal eighth-grade picture, not that awful fifth-grade one). The words "Lilly's Lesbian Diary" sort of danced across the top.

There was only one entry:

> *Hi! Welcome to my blog. My name is Lilly and I'm an eighth grader at Truman Middle School. I've decided it's time to come out of the closet and tell everyone that I am a total lesbian. And I'm proud of it. I'm going to use this blog to write about all my lesbian experiences.*

I stared in horror at the computer screen. I didn't write this. I didn't write any of it. I wasn't a-a . . . *lesbian!* I didn't even know any lesbians, except for maybe Emily Tate. Everyone said she was one.

I kept reading:

> *Here's my list of the top five girls I want to go out with:*
> 5. *Morgan Kennedy*
> 4. *Kylie Holtzman*
> 3. *Cassie Wheeler*
> 2. *Brianna Brinkman*
> *And the number one girl I want to go out with is . . . .(drumroll please!)*
> 1. *Hayley Wood*

All popular girls!

"Lilly?" my mom called. "Where are you?"

"I-I'm right here," I called back, hoping my voice didn't give anything away. I quickly shut everything down and tried to act normal when she came out, but it was hard. My entire body trembled. My heart pounded so hard I thought it was going to explode.

"What are you doing?" Mom asked. "Are you on the computer?"

"Yeah . . . I was just . . . checking Centerpoint . . . to make sure I got all my homework."

My mom looked at me funny, like she didn't quite believe me.

I stood up. "I better get ready for school now," I said. Even though school was the last place I wanted to go.

How in the world was I going to face everyone at school?

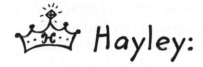

Brianna:

I checked the Truth about Truman website while
I dried my hair before school. Lilly's "secret" was up:
LILLY CLARKE IS A LEZBO! There was a link to her
diary, which was all about her "lesbian experiences." Plus
a list of girls she "likes." Hayley and I were at the top of
the list.

Hayley was going to FREAK OUT when she saw this.

I turned my hair dryer off and checked my buddy
list to see if Hayley was online. She wasn't, so I grabbed
my cell phone and texted a quick message to her: go 2
truth about t. then call me.

I had a feeling Lilly's days in our group were numbered.

Hayley:

I got Brianna's text message just as I was turning on
my computer. I had already been planning on checking
out that site, but thanks anyway, Brianna.

I rubbed foundation makeup into my face while I
waited for the page to load. There it was: *LILLY CLARKE
IS A LEZBO! Don't believe me? Click here to read Lilly's
blog. Find out who she's in love with.*

I wiped my fingers on a tissue, then clicked on the
link, which led me to this purple website that was all
about how Lilly likes *girls.* There was even a list of all the

girls she likes on there. *Our entire group was on that list!* And *I* was number one.

There were seven comments about all this on the Truth about Truman. Most of them said things like, "They're ALL a bunch of lezzies!"

I gasped. Who said that?

Somebody who called themselves Megagulp, but who was Megagulp?

Okay, we needed to do some serious damage control. We couldn't have people thinking our group was made up of *lesbians!*

This was when I started having some doubts about Lilly. Whether she was gay or not, that was her business. But beyond that, there was something else that was bothering me: People didn't respect her anymore. And if they didn't respect her, they wouldn't respect us.

I didn't have all my makeup on yet, but I picked up my phone and called Brianna anyway. We had to figure out what we were going to do about this. And we had to figure it out before school.

 Trevor:

Just because it said on that website that Lilly Clarke was gay didn't mean she really was. Kids have been saying that about me since third grade, and believe me, *I'm* not gay!

I didn't even know what gay or queer or homo

meant when I first heard those insults in third grade. I thought queer meant weird. Even back then, there was something about me that was different from the other kids. I didn't walk like them; I didn't talk like them; and I've never been into sports or bands or movie stars. So by everyone else's definition, I guess I was weird.

I looked up homo at dictionary.com and found out it was short for homosexual. Then when I read the definition, I had sort of this *aha* moment. Not about myself, though. About my Uncle Cole and Uncle Mike. Uncle Cole is my mom's brother. Uncle Mike is the guy he lives with. In a one-bedroom apartment.

Were Uncle Cole and Uncle Mike *homosexuals*? I asked my mom back in third grade. She wanted to know where I heard that word. I didn't want to tell her kids at school had called *me* that, so I told her I read it in a book.

She said yes, Uncle Cole and Uncle Mike were homosexuals, but *gay* was a better word. Then she asked if I understood what that meant. I don't know if I really understood yet back then, but I said I did because I didn't want to talk about it anymore. Uncle Cole and Uncle Mike were two of my favorite people in the whole world. (They still are!) I didn't want to think about them being weird or different.

As I got older, I realized they really weren't all that different from anyone else. Not in any way that actually mattered. And Uncle Cole is one of the few connections I have to Mom, so I'd have to be really stupid to think it mattered that he was gay.

But when you're in middle school, it matters a lot if you're gay. It matters a lot if people just *think* you're gay. It's like one of the worst things you can say about someone in middle school.

 Amr:

Whoa. If there's one thing that makes people more nervous than Muslims, it's people who are gay. At least in middle school. I don't think there's ever been a popular gay person in the history of middle school.

Lilly was going to have a hard time getting past this. At our school, if people even *think* you're gay, you may as well be gay.

 Zebby:

At first I thought I was on the website Amr made for his mom's garden club last year because the background and layout were exactly the same. But then I actually read the words: Lilly's Lesbian Diary.

Lilly was a lesbian? Really? And even if she was, *that* was the big secret?

I'll admit, part of me wondered if it was true. I mean, how could someone as boy crazy as Lilly turn out to be gay? But what did I know? Maybe she just acted all boy crazy to cover up the fact she was gay. Or maybe she wasn't gay at all. Maybe milkandhoney, whoever he, she, or they were, made it all up? I was pretty sure *somebody* had made up that whole diary thing. Who calls a diary "My LESBIAN diary?" Would a real lesbian do that? I don't think so.

But even if Lilly was a lesbian, so what? This was the twenty-first century. Most people don't care if a person is gay or not. Well . . . most of the people *I* hang out with don't care.

As it turned out, some people did care. A lot. And of course Hayley just made things worse by telling anyone who would listen that of course *she* wasn't gay. You should have seen her. She was practically holding court on the steps of the school.

"I am *not* gay!" she said. "I had no idea that Lilly was. This whole thing is just really embarrassing for me."

Leave it to Hayley to turn herself into the victim. Please! There were so many more important things to worry about at our school than whether or not Lilly Clarke was gay.

You're probably wondering if I ever thought about just taking the link to Lilly's Lesbian Diary down. After all, one of the two rules we had for the site said that what you posted had to be true. And honestly, I didn't know if this was true. I didn't know whether Lilly was gay.

But I didn't know that it *wasn't* true, either. Obviously somebody thought it was. That's why they posted that link. And really, it was just a link. One little link wasn't so bad.

We also said that anyone could post whatever they

wanted on our site and we wouldn't censor it. So . . . in the interest of free speech, I decided I had to leave that link up.

 ## Lilly:

Hayley's mom called my mom again that morning. She couldn't pick me up for school because Hayley had to get there early to make up her P.E.

Right. Hayley hadn't missed any school lately, so I knew she didn't have any P.E. to make up. Hayley and the others were avoiding me again. Because of that new website that wasn't even mine.

When I got to school, I didn't have the nerve to check the bathroom to see if my friends were in there. If they were, they'd probably ignore me. That's what we do when we push someone out of our group.

Not knowing what else to do, I went straight to my homeroom.

"Lilly!" Mrs. Connor jumped when I walked in. She'd been correcting homework or something at her desk.

"Hi, Mrs. Connor," I mumbled. I figured she'd go back to whatever she was doing and I'd . . . take out my math and start on the next day's assignment. Since Mrs. Connor was also my math teacher and all.

But I could feel Mrs. Connor's eyes on me as I opened my math book. "Is everything all right, Lilly?"

she asked with concern.

Oh, no. Did *Mrs. Connor* go on that website?

I cleared my throat. "Everything's fine, Mrs. Connor."

"Good. I've never known you to arrive so early for class." Mrs. Connor smiled. "I got a little worried."

I forced myself to smile back, then went back to my assignment.

It was worse when other kids started arriving. I could tell by all the whispering and snickering, and the way people looked at me, then looked away that a lot of people had seen that new website. And they all thought it was true!

What was I going to do?

Cassie was the only one from our group who was in my homeroom. Cassie scurried in about five seconds before the bell rang, slid into her seat across the aisle from me, then turned her whole body away from me.

When the bell rang for first period, Cassie leapt out of her chair and hurried out the door. She went across the hall and waited for Brianna and Morgan to come out of Mr. Wesack's homeroom. Brianna kind of smirked at me, then the three of them strolled down the hall without me.

I'M NOT GAY! I wanted to shout after them. I have a boyfriend! A cool one, too. And everyone knew it, so why—

That was it! All I had to do was remind everyone about me and Reece. We had to be seen walking through the halls together (preferably holding hands). That would fix everything.

After fourth period, I waited outside the cafeteria for Reece. People kept staring at me as they filed past. "Lezbo!" some of them whispered under their breath. Others oinked at me. Just like they used to do in fifth grade. Then I saw Hayley and Brianna. They turned their heads like they didn't even know me. I swallowed hard and tried to act like it didn't matter. But I was having a hard time keeping myself together.

Come on, Reece! I thought, biting my lip. Hurry up! I knew Reece was coming from P.E.; how long did it take to get from the gym to the cafeteria anyway?

Finally, I spotted him in a crowd of boys making their way to the cafeteria. He said something to Josh Schumaker and Josh laughed. I don't think either of them noticed me standing there at first.

I stood on my tiptoes to get their attention. "Reece!" I cried, waving my hand.

He stopped for a second and his smile sort of froze on his face. Josh leaned over and whispered something, to Reece and Reece nodded. Then Reece hurried away and Josh moved toward me.

"Reece, wait!" I called, trying to get over to him, but Josh stood right in my way.

"I—uh—don't think you guys are going out any-more," Josh informed me.

What?

"Don't look so surprised," Josh said with a mean grin. "You like girls better anyway."

"But I don't!" I said. "That website, it's not true!"

Josh just walked away.

Then I noticed Sara Murphy leaning against the opposite wall, hugging her books to her chest. She just stood there, *watching* me. Didn't I have enough problems?

"What are you looking at?" I asked.

But I forgot. She doesn't talk.

I just shook my head and walked away. I spent the rest of the lunch period in our old bathroom.

Reece:

Hayley asked me if I wrote about what happened for the website. I said no. I just wrote what I had to for language arts and that was it. But Hayley said I had a unique perspective and I should write about it for the website, too. I don't know what she's talking about. I don't have a unique perspective. And none of that stuff really affected me much. I was busy with football.

But Hayley said I should at least write about how me and Lilly broke up. So okay, Lilly and I broke up. And yeah, *I* broke up with *her*. I don't really have anything else to say about it than that. Can you blame me for breaking up with her? People were saying she was gay! Would you want to go out with a girl who was gay?

All that other stuff, though, that stuff with the computer? I don't know anything about that. I only went on that Truth about Truman website a couple times. There wasn't much about football on it, so I didn't think it was very interesting.

? Anonymous:

In language arts last year, Mrs. Jonstone said there's nothing more powerful than the written word. I never really believed it then, but I was starting to believe it now. People were looking at Lilly Clarke a lot differently now. All because of a few things they saw about her online. This was working out way better than I ever thought it would.

 Lilly:

I was never so relieved to hear the bell ring at the end of the day as I was that day.

Hayley, Brianna and I were supposed to go over to Brianna's house after school to work on our cheers, but considering Hayley and Brianna hadn't said a word to me all day, it was probably safe to assume we weren't practicing today. Or, that *I* wasn't practicing with them.

So how was I supposed to get home if I didn't get a ride from Brianna's mom? Since my mom worked, I always got a ride from Hayley or Brianna's mom. I couldn't very well call my mom at work and tell her I didn't have a ride today. She'd want to know why and I couldn't tell her why. So what was I supposed to do? Walk?

I'd never walked home from school before, but it wasn't far. Zebby and Amr walked to and from school all the time. But then again, people like them always walked (or rode their bikes) everywhere they went. People in my crowd got rides.

I felt weird walking home. Like everyone was looking at me and wondering why I was walking. Or why I was walking by myself. *Don't you have any friends?* they probably wondered. I don't remember the last time I went anywhere by myself.

Some kids in the back seat of a blue car rolled down their window and yelled, "Hey, Lezzie!" as they drove past me.

I didn't even know them.

I tried to avoid looking at any other cars that went by after that. But at the same time, I sort of watched out of the corner of my eye for Brianna's mom's car. I wondered what Brianna's mom would do if she saw me walking? Would she stop to offer me a ride? Or would Brianna and everyone have already warned her not to?

But I never saw their car the whole way home. Brianna didn't live in my neighborhood.

When I got home, I went straight to the computer. Wow! I had thirty-seven emails, which had to be some sort of record. Most of them came from stupid addresses like fatuglyandproud@yahoo.com, or ohbaby325@hotmail.com so there was no way to know who any of these people were.

I clicked on the first one. *YOU'RE SUCH A POSER!!!!* it said in huge letters. That was it.

I deleted it.

The next one said: *Dear Lilly, You're so disgusting. You walk around like you're better than everyone. And then we all find out you're a homo!*

But I'm not, I thought, blinking back tears. Why does everyone believe that stupid website?

My hands shook as I scrolled through the list of emails. Were all these emails like those first two? I scanned the list of email addresses, searching for names or addresses of people I knew. But the only one in there that was even close to something I recognized was emilythelesbiantate@hotmail.com.

That couldn't really be Emily Tate's email address, and Emily certainly wasn't a friend of mine, so I don't know why I clicked on the email. But I did. *Dear Lilly, I want you so bad—*

Ew! I stopped reading there. I clicked delete about ten times.

 **Trevor:**

"Psst!" Reece Weber hissed during math.

I didn't think he was talking to me, so I ignored him. We were supposed to be taking a test.

I felt a pencil jab me in the neck. "Hey, Loser!" Reece whispered.

I continued to ignore him, but then OW! It felt like

the pencil had gone all the way through my skin and into my bone.

"Hey," Reece whispered again as I massaged my throbbing neck. "I'm talking to you."

I whirled around. "Knock it off!" I whispered back.

"Then move over," Reece said, trying to see around me. "I can't see your answers."

"You're not supposed to see my answers," I muttered under my breath.

By now the kids on either side of us were watching us. But Mr. Wesack was too busy on his computer to pay any attention to what was going on.

I scooted my desk forward as far as I could without bumping into Cassie Wheeler's desk in front of me. Then I hunched over my test and tried to concentrate on the problem I'd been working on:

$X + 12\ 1/3 = 25.$ *Solve for X.*

How was I supposed to solve for X when I kept feeling a pencil jabbing into me? It was like a little woodpecker pecking away at me. First my neck. Then my right shoulder blade. Then my left shoulder blade. Then the neck again. Then my middle. Peck! Peck! Peck!

Finally, I couldn't take it anymore. "KNOCK IT OFF!" I yelled, spinning around in my chair. I yanked the pencil out of Reece's hand, snapped it in two, then slammed the pieces into his chest.

I have to tell you, I've never done anything like that before.

Reece's eyes grew wide with shock. I was pretty shocked myself.

"What's going on back there?" Mr. Wesack asked. Sure, *now* he pays attention.

Reece managed to find his voice before I did. "Trevor just went psycho on me," he said all innocent. "He grabbed the pencil out of my hand and broke it and threw it at me."

"That's because he's been poking me with it all period!" I defended myself. "He was trying to get me to move so he could copy off me."

"I was not," Reece argued. "Why would I copy off of him? He's a moron!"

Moron? I wasn't a straight-A student, but I was a lot smarter than Reece.

Mr. Wesack got up from his desk and moved toward us. The little vein above his right ear pulsed.

"Hey!" I cried when Mr. Wesack yanked the test out from under my hand. He took Reece's test, too. Then he put both tests together and tore them down the middle. We were both getting zeros.

It wasn't fair! I'd studied for this test and everything. And I hadn't even done anything wrong. I was just trying to take the test.

Mr. Wesack pulled two green passes out of his front pocket and used my desk to fill them out.

"You two can go and visit with Mrs. Horton for the rest of the period." Mr. Wesack handed me the first pass.

He wasn't just taking our tests, he was making us go see Mrs. H., too? All because I broke Reece's pencil?

"We don't tolerate fighting or cheating here at Truman," Mr. Wesack said.

I wasn't fighting OR cheating. But it didn't matter. I took the pass, grabbed my stuff and hurried out the door.

"Hey, Loser! Wait up!" Reece called as he tried to catch up to me. I started walking faster.

I got to Mrs. Horton's office about a second and a half before Reece did, but Mrs. Horton still called Reece into her office before she called me in. Figures, I thought, slumping onto the hard wood bench outside her office. Jocks always got special treatment around here.

Reece was in there about ten minutes before the door opened again. "Thanks, Mrs. Horton," he said with a big grin.

Thanks, Mrs. Horton?

"You can come in now, Trevor," Mrs. Horton said.

I stood up, but waited for Reece to move past me before I went in there. As I expected, he rammed his shoulder into mine when he passed. "Oh, sorry," he said all wide-eyed and innocent.

I went into Mrs. Horton's office and nudged the door closed with my foot.

"Sit down, Trevor," Mrs. Horton said in a tired voice. I sat.

"I understand you and Reece had a little problem in Mr. Wesack's class?" she asked.

"Actually, I think Reece was the one with the problem."

"What do you mean?"

"I was just trying to take my test, but he kept poking me with his pencil."

Mrs. Horton cocked her head. "Reece poked you with his pencil?" I could tell she didn't believe me. "Why would he do that?"

Why is the sky blue?

"I mean, what were you doing to provoke him?" Mrs. Horton clarified.

Here we go again. "Taking my test!" I said. Hadn't I just said that?

"Don't raise your voice, Trevor."

I wasn't raising my voice. But I repeated what I said in a softer voice just to make Mrs. Horton happy. "I was just taking my test."

"That's not what Reece said."

Of course it wasn't. Who cared what Reece said? It wasn't the truth.

I wanted to reach across Mrs. Horton's wide desk, grab her by the shoulders, and shake her. How come anytime I had trouble with some other kid, it was always, "Well, what are *you* doing to provoke it, Trevor?"

Did anyone ever ask Lilly Clarke what *she* did to provoke everyone?

 Zebby:

We had some more updating to do on our site. I knew I wouldn't be able to do it at my house because my dad was working from home that day. But Hayley and Brianna were hanging out in the media center after school. Again. So I asked Amr if I could go to his house and work on his computer while he and his mom prayed.

He said I could, so I went up to his room by myself.

His computer was on. In fact, our website was already up. We had quite a few new things on the site: an article on the Lego robotics club (which was good!), three new bad teacher stories, a "letter to the editor" that suggested the popular girls were all a bunch of lezzies (sigh), a stupid-looking comic of two girls kissing (double sigh), and more than a hundred comments on milkandhoney's "announcement" about Lilly (triple sigh). I needed to move a few things around to make the site look better. But I was so depressed about the kind of stuff that got people talking on this site that I just sat there and stared at Amr's computer screen for a while.

I really didn't mean to snoop, but while I was staring at the screen, I noticed a tab for this other window on Amr's computer. The tab said, "A Little Fable."

Amr wrote a fable? Was he planning on putting it on the site? Amr's a computer guy. He deals in facts and logic. If you want a step-by-step how-to-do-something sort of article, Amr's the guy to write it. But creative writing (like fables!)? That's not Amr.

I wanted to see what kind of fable he'd written. I didn't think he'd mind . . . until I actually saw the fable.

A Little Fable
By milkandhoney
*Once upon a time there was a dog named
Lilly. She wasn't pretty, she wasn't funny, and
she didn't have any special talents. In fact, there
were no good qualities about her whatsoever.*

But for some reason all the popular dogs let her hang around with them. (Popular dogs don't need a reason . . . they just like something because it's "popular.")

But one day, one of the popular dogs (let's call her Athena because Athena is the Goddess of Wisdom) said, "Why do we even hang around with Lilly? She's just bringing us down."

The other popular dogs thought about it and they realized Athena was right. So from that day forward, NOBODY liked Lilly Clarke anymore.

I could hardly believe my eyes. *Amr* was milkand-honey???

 Lilly:

Someone was setting me up. Someone was trying to turn the whole school against me. The question was who?

It had to be Zebby and Amr. No one else hated me as much as they did.

Zebby swore it wasn't them. But if it wasn't her and Amr, who else could it be? Who else would want to turn the whole school against me? Who else would even dare take on someone in my group?

Could it be someone who was already *in* my group? Someone who wanted me gone from the group, but they couldn't just kick me out because I was close to Hayley. Someone like . . . Brianna?

Brianna and I have never really liked each other much. We just sort of put up with each other because of Hayley. To tell you the truth, I wouldn't mind if *she* got bumped from our group. Was it possible she felt the same way about me?

If she got to talking with someone who went to Hoover, she could have found out I used to be sort of fat in elementary school. She could have gotten a copy of my old school picture from anyone who had a memory book.

I wouldn't have thought she was smart enough to scan a picture in and upload it to a website, or set up an anonymous email address or a blog that was supposedly my diary. But everyone knew her stepbrother was some kind of genius. He could have helped her.

All of a sudden, I heard a knocking sound coming from my computer. One of my friends was logging on to instant messaging. I switched windows to see who it was. It was Gymnasticsqueen. Hayley.

I swallowed hard. I wondered what would happen if I tried messaging her? She'd probably ignore me, like she did at school. But at least with instant messaging, you can still talk to someone, even if they're not talking to you, and maybe they'll at least read what you wrote?

I double-clicked on her name and typed, "hi." *What else did I want to say to her?*

A few seconds later Gymnasticsqueen wrote back. "hi."

Oh! She was speaking to me?

"i thought u were mad at me," I typed. "r u mad?"
I didn't even wait for an answer, I just kept on typing.
"i didn't write any of that stuff on that website. that's not
my diary!!! please, hayley, you've got to believe me!"

"i'm not mad," Hayley typed back.

I waited for her to say more. Like whether she
believed me or not, or whether or not we were still
friends. But she didn't.

"someone (milkandhoney!) is trying to turn everyone against me," I typed. "they r saying stuff about me
that isn't true. i'm NOT gay!"

"then why would someone say that you are?"

She was asking *me?* "i told you. someone's trying to
turn everyone against me."

"who would do that?"

"i don't know. i've wondered if it's . . . brianna." It
would be interesting to see what Hayley said about that.

"brianna? what makes u think it's brianna?"

Well . . . "i don't think she likes me very much. i
think she thinks i stole you from her or something, and i
think she'd do anything to turn you against me."

I waited and waited, but Hayley didn't say anything
more.

"hello???" I typed. "hayley? r u still there?"

"hayley's here," someone typed a couple seconds
later. "and I'm here with her. hello, lilly. it's me . . .
BRIANNA!"

O.M.G.!

 *Amr:*

My mom had just baked a fresh batch of pita chips
with olive oil and herbs, so when I finished praying, I
grabbed a bowl of chips, then headed up to my room.
I could tell something was wrong the minute I walked
in. Zebby was all slouched in my chair with her arms
crossed, the blue of her hair hanging around her face.

"What?" I asked, handing her the bowl of chips.

She didn't take it, so I set the bowl down on my desk
and asked again, "What?" Louder this time.

"You're milkandhoney," she said. It wasn't a question;
it was a statement.

At first I didn't know what she was talking about.
Milk and honey? Then I saw what she had up on my
computer.

"Oh, that," I said. "I didn't write that."

Zebby cocked her head at me.

"I didn't! I saw it on our site this morning and . . .
I took it down."

"Right," Zebby said with a snort. "So tell me, Amr,
what made you decide to take it down?"

She had to ask? "Well, because it isn't very nice," I said.

"There's other stuff on our site that *isn't very nice*,
too," Zebby said, rising to her feet. "Why would you take
this down and not anything else?"

"I, uh—" I shifted my weight from one foot to the
other, not knowing what to say. She had a point. "How

could you think *I'm* milkandhoney?" I cried.

Zebby started listing things off on her fingers. "Well, this fable, to start with. I was on the site this morning, too, Amr. This wasn't up there. Second, you still have your fifth-grade memory book, so you could've scanned that picture of Lilly and put it up on our website. Third, nobody knows more about computers than you do. You could set things up so no one, not even me, could trace the name milkandhoney back to you. But you made one mistake, Amr. Which brings me to number four: you used the same background to create Lilly's Lesbian Diary as you used on your mom's garden club's website!"

Zebby, my best and oldest friend, was calling me a liar. And a bully.

I cleared my throat. "Well, that's interesting," I said calmly. "Because lately I've been wondering if *you* were milkandhoney."

"Me?" She stepped back.

"Sure. I know for a fact you still have your fifth-grade memory book, too. You know as much about scanning and uploading as I do. You're pretty artistic; you could've drawn all that stuff all over her picture. You know where I got that template for my mom's garden club's website, so you could've used it to create Lilly's Lesbian Diary, too. And nobody has a bigger grudge against Lilly Clarke than you do."

Zebby opened her mouth, but then closed it again before any more words came out. She pushed past me, stormed down the hall, down the stairs, and out my front door, which she slammed closed behind her.

Brianna:

"I can't believe she said that about you. Can you?" Hayley asked after we closed her instant messaging program.

I plopped down on Hayley's bed and put my feet up against her headboard. "Yes," I said. "I totally believe it. Lilly's always talking about people behind their backs. She says stuff about you when you're not around, too, you know."

"She does?" Hayley looked surprised.

"Of course she does!"

"What does she say?"

Well, Lilly usually didn't say much about Hayley *to me*, but that was because Lilly and I didn't usually spend much time alone together. I was pretty sure Lilly said things about Hayley to other people, though. I mean, everybody talks about people behind their backs.

"It's okay, Brianna," Hayley said, sitting down next to me. "I know you don't want to hurt my feelings, but you can tell me. I want to know what she said."

I had to tell her something, so I said, "Well . . . she thinks you're bossy." Everyone thinks Hayley's bossy. "And that you're . . . well, kind of full of yourself."

Hayley stiffened. "Anything else?"

"I don't know. Not really."

She got up and wandered over to her dresser. I watched as she picked up tubes of lipstick, then set them back down again.

"I don't know what to think about Lilly anymore, Brianna," Hayley said finally. "She's not the person I thought she was."

"Me either," I said.

"What do you think we should do about it?"

She was asking *me?* I shrugged. "What do *you* think we should do about it?"

"Well, obviously we can't keep hanging around with her. I think we're going to have to cut her loose."

It was about time.

Zebby:

I couldn't believe *Amr* was milkandhoney. Amr was one of the nicest people I knew. He was always so calm and easygoing. He never said anything bad about anyone else. That just goes to show you can never really know a person.

It had been two years since Lilly dumped us. Even though I didn't even want to be friends with Lilly anymore, I had to admit it still hurt. It didn't hurt as much as it did back in sixth grade, but it hurt. Probably because she was so nasty about it. If she had just stopped hanging out with us that would've been one thing. But no, she had to show off to her new friends and say mean things about us to prove she wasn't our friend anymore. Things like, "*Zebby and Amr?* No, they're not my friends. I only hung out with them a little bit in elementary school. And I only did it because my mom made me."

FYI . . . her mom was such a mess when Lilly's dad left that that were some days she never even got out of bed. Her mom was in no condition to *make her* do anything.

Lilly called me Grease Girl in sixth grade because my hair wasn't always squeaky clean. And I remember once she even called Amr a terrorist. That was the worst thing.

I got really mad about that, but Amr said, "Let it go, Zebby. It's not worth getting upset about."

But apparently, he *was* upset. More upset than I would have guessed. And now he was getting his revenge.

So what was I going to do about it?

 Lilly:

All my friends were ignoring me at school. How could I have gone from "popular girl" to social outcast so fast?

Nobody was talking to me at school, but they sure were emailing me. Every time I got on the computer, I had several new messages. Most were from made-up email addresses, and most were messages telling me how ugly I was, what a hypocrite I was, or what a poser I was. One even said they wished I would die.

Delete . . . Delete . . . Delete . . .

"Lilly, are you on the computer again?" my mom asked.

I jumped when I heard her voice. My mom was like a cat sometimes—you never heard her coming. I quickly closed my email program and my web browser and tried to act normal.

"What are you doing?" Mom asked, peering at the plain background that was up on the computer.

I shrugged. "School stuff." It wasn't a total lie.

Mom frowned. "What kind of school stuff?" She stepped closer to the computer. "Why did you close everything up when I walked into the room?"

I couldn't deal with my mother on top of everything else. Not now. "Why do you have to know what I'm doing every single second of the day?" I asked. Then I hit the power button and stormed off to my room.

I tried to slam the door shut behind me, but Mom caught it before it closed and pushed her way into my room.

"Can't I get any privacy around here?" I cried as I flopped onto my bed. I rolled over so I was facing my wall instead of my mother.

"No," Mom said. "Not when you act like this."

"Like what?"

Mom sat down beside me. She touched my shoulder. "What's going on, Lilly? Why are you being so secretive?"

"I'm not!" I wiggled out from under her grasp and tears sprang to my eyes. *Do not cry*, I told myself, blinking them away.

"Yes, you are. And whatever it is, I think it has something to do with the computer. You're always using the computer, and then you shut everything down whenever I walk into the room."

I clamped my jaws together. I couldn't talk about this. Not with her. Not with anyone.

"You're not talking to some stranger online, are you?" Mom asked.

What? "No!" I cried.

"I hope not. I hope you know better than to get involved with people you don't know online, because that can be really dangerous."

"I know," I said into my comforter. What? Did she think I was five years old?

Mom sighed. "Then what is it? Tell me!"

But I couldn't tell her. I couldn't tell anyone.

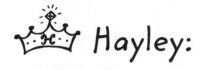 Hayley:

We were pretty sure Lilly would get the hint eventually and realize she wasn't in our group anymore. But she'd already tried instant messaging me, and even though she seemed to know better than to sit with us at lunch, she still kept staring at me in school. It was like she was obsessed with me or something. *Ew! What if she really* was *gay?*

"What if Lilly shows up at the football game on Friday ready to cheer with us?" Brianna asked when we were hanging out at my house after school.

I didn't think Lilly would really do that . . . but what if she did? That would be so embarrassing. For all of us. We had already replaced her with Cassie. And I don't want to be mean, but Cassie's a much better cheerleader than Lilly ever was. She shouts louder and jumps higher, and well, she makes Brianna and me look good.

"What can we do to make sure Lilly doesn't show up on Friday?" I asked. We couldn't exactly go over to her house and take away her cheerleading uniform and pompoms.

"Hey, I know!" Brianna said. "We could, like, pretend to be Reece or Austin or somebody else on the football team, and we could send her an email that says 'please don't cheer for us because people will laugh at us if we have lesbian cheerleaders.'"

Hmm. Now *there* was an idea!

So we wrote the email together. It was kind of fun to pretend we were guys. Brianna and I laughed and laughed as we reread what we wrote in deep, guy voices. You know, with lots of grunts and stuff. All I can say is, thank goodness for email! It's so much nicer to drop someone by email than in person.

 Lilly:

I checked the Truth about Truman website the next morning while my mom was in the shower. Whew! Nothing new.

Then I checked my email. I deleted seven nasty emails without reading them. I was about to delete the one from "ten-concerned-football-players," but then I saw Reece's name at the bottom, so I went back and read the whole email: *Dear Lilly, Yo! We don't want you cheering at our games no more. It's embarrassing. None of the other schools have any lezzie cheerleaders. We don't want no lezzie cheerleaders either, you ugly cow!* It was supposedly signed by all the eighth-grade varsity football players.

Was this for real? Or had Hayley and Brianna written it to kick me off the cheerleading squad? Was there any way to find out?

I clicked my instant message program and waited to see if anyone was online.

I drew in my breath. Hayley was.

What could I possibly say to her? Dear Hayley. Please be my friend again. That sounded so desperate.

Well, I *was* desperate. So I double clicked on her user name, then typed, *Can we talk?*

But a new window popped up. It said: *This user has blocked you from instant messaging.*

I guess that answered my question.

 Zebby:

Every time I passed Amr in the hall, he looked like he wanted to shoot me full of poison arrow darts. And Amr was not normally a violent person.

What was the deal? Why was *he* mad at *me*? It wasn't like I'd turned him in.

If anyone had a right to be mad around here, it was

me. Amr lied to me. He *lied* to me! And then *he* accused *me* of being milkandhoney.

I was so mad at him, I went to the media center after school so I wouldn't have to see him walking on the other side of the street.

"Zebby! Hey, how are you doing?" Mrs. Conway asked when I walked in. She had a small stack of books in her arms.

"Okay. Do you need any help putting books away?" I asked.

"Well," Mrs. Conway said, gazing off into the 500s. "This is all I have left. Trevor and Sara have gotten every- thing else put away already." I could see Trevor putting away paperbacks and Sara pushing in chairs.

The two of them were *always* in the media center after school! Every single day. Didn't they have lives?

"I could still put those books away for you," I said. I really didn't want to run into Amr on the way home from school.

"Okay," Mrs. Conway said, setting the books in my arms.

It didn't take me very long to put them away. "Is there anything else I can do?" I asked Mrs. Conway when I finished.

"I don't think so, honey. But thank you."

I nodded, then started to walk away. But before I reached the door, Mrs. Conway asked, "Is everything all right, Zebby? You seem kind of down."

I *was* down. And if there was anybody at school I could talk to about my problems, Mrs. Conway was it. But I didn't know if she even knew about the Truth about Truman. And I didn't feel right talking to her about Amr.

"I'm fine, Mrs. Conway. Just tired," I said.

I'd figure out what, if anything, to do about Amr on my own.

 ## Lilly:

I have never in my life felt so alone. I went entire days without saying a word to anyone until six o'clock when my mom got home from work. And even then, there were days I spoke fewer than seventeen words out loud: "Yes. No. No. I'm fine. I have a lot of homework. Yes. I'm tired. Good night." That was all I said one day. I was like that weird girl who never talked. Except at the moment, I think even *she* was more popular than I was.

It just didn't end! People called me names, whispered about me, or just plain ignored me at school. But then it was almost worse when I went home, because people would email me and IM me nonstop. I just couldn't get away from it.

Then one day, a whole new thing went up on the Truth about Truman.com: *If you liked Lilly's Lesbian Diary, wait until you see what I'm going to post later tonight. —milkandhoney.*

Oh, no. *Now* what?

? Anonymous:

If you liked Lilly's Lesbian Diary, wait until you see what I'm going to post later tonight. —milkandhoney.
Wait a minute! *I'm* milkandhoney, and I didn't post that!!! Who's posting stuff with my name?

 Lilly:

I kept waiting for milkandhoney to post whatever they were going to post, but they didn't post it before my mom got home from work. And then once she was home, she totally guarded the computer. I couldn't get on it the rest of the night. Well, no way was I going to school the next day without knowing ahead of time what milkandhoney had posted. So I set my alarm for two o'clock in the morning. It turned out I didn't need the alarm. I never actually went to sleep.

At two A.M., I slid out from under my covers and crept over to my door. I opened it slowly, quietly, and tiptoed out into the hall. I hardly breathed as I inched across the hall and pressed my ear against my mom's door. I could hear her snoring in there, so I continued on to the living room. I turned on the computer, which, let me tell you, sounds really LOUD when it roars to life at two o'clock in the morning. The screen seems extra bright at that hour, too.

Squinting against the brightness, I typed in www. truthabouttruman.com and waited for the site to come up. I dreaded seeing what was on there now.

It was just one line again: *Click HERE for something interesting.*

I clicked and was immediately taken to a brand new website. A We Hate Lilly Clarke website.

How much do you hate Lilly Clarke? Tell us in 250 words or less. The winner will receive $5!!!!

Five dollars? For writing about how much you hate me?

Who posted this website? Who was judging the entries and awarding the prize? I couldn't tell.

But there were already five entries. I couldn't stand to read them.

 Anonymous:

I admit, I did the other stuff. I posted the picture of Lilly. I doctored it up a day later. I did the Lilly's Lesbian Diary website. I posted some sort of mean comments on the Truth about Truman, and I sent Lilly a bunch of emails under the name "milkandhoney." If I had thought about starting a "We Hate Lilly" website, I might have done that, too. But I didn't; I swear I didn't!

 # Zebby:

How much do you hate Lilly Clarke?

Was this *really* Amr? Even if he did hate Lilly, it was hard to imagine him putting up a site like this. This was like . . . terrorism. And Amr was sensitive about terrorism.

Which made me wonder: what if Amr *wasn't* milkandhoney? Was it possible he wasn't?

There was an easy way to find out. Amr claimed that fable had been up on our site earlier that day. I had been on the site earlier that morning, too, and I never saw it. That was why I didn't believe him when he said he took it down. But what if he was on *before* I was? Or after I was? All I had to do was check the history of our site to find out for sure.

So I did.

And guess what I found. That fable was up on our site for about twenty minutes that morning. I felt lower than I've ever felt in my life.

Amr had been telling the truth. Somebody else posted that fable. He took it down. And I didn't believe him.

No wonder he was so mad at me. What kind of friend was I?

I picked up the phone and dialed Amr's number. His mom answered the phone.

"Hello, Zebby," she said. "I am sorry, but Amr is not here. He has gone out to breakfast with his father."

"Could I get his dad's cell phone number? I really need to talk to him."

Amr's mom gave me the number. I called it, but there was no answer. Maybe Amr's dad just couldn't hear his cell phone wherever he was.

Or . . . maybe Amr was avoiding me.

 Lilly:

"I don't feel so good," I moaned when my mom came in to wake me up. I really didn't feel good because I'd hardly slept all night. Plus I'd just spent the last fifteen minutes holding my comforter over my head. So my head was all sweaty, and it was hard to get enough air.

"What's the matter?" Mom asked gently.

I put on my most pathetic face. "My head hurts. So does my stomach. And so does my throat." Why not cover all the bases?

Mom leaned over and felt my forehead. "You are a little warm," she said. "I'll go get the thermometer."

She came back in about two minutes with an old-fashioned thermometer that you have to hold in your mouth. "Open up," she said, sticking the thermometer in. Then she went to put in her contacts.

There was one good thing about those old style thermometers. If you can get ten seconds alone with one . . . just you, the thermometer, and a light bulb, you can give yourself a fever as high as you want. So as soon as my mom left, I rolled over toward my bedside light and held the thermometer against the bulb. As soon as the silver stuff reached 102 degrees, I stuck the thermometer back in my mouth.

Good thing, too, because I could hear my mom coming back. She grabbed the thermometer from my lips, peered down at it, and frowned. "Looks like you really are sick."

Yes!

Mom sighed again. "Do you need me to stay home with you?" She looked a little worried that I was going to say yes.

"No, that's okay," I moaned. I knew it was hard for Mom to get the time off. And I really didn't want her to stay home with me, anyway. I wanted to be alone.

Mom came back at noon to check on me. She also brought me some chicken noodle soup from Panera, which tasted so good I ate all four servings of it. I told her I was okay, but still feeling crummy. That way I was setting the stage for staying home tomorrow, too. Maybe even the next day. In fact, maybe I'd *never* go back to school.

 # Amr:

"Amr!" I heard Zebby calling me between first and second period. "Amr, wait up!"

But I didn't wait. I had nothing to say to Zebby Bower. And eventually, she lost me in the crowd.

She tried to catch me again between third and fourth period, but this time I escaped to the bathroom.

I figured she'd be looking for me in the cafeteria, too, so I decided to go to the pool and swim laps during lunch. When I got out of the pool and went into the locker room, there was Zebby sitting on one of the benches between the rows of lockers.

Unbelievable! "This is the *boys'* locker room," I informed her as I wrapped my towel around my waist.

"So?"

"So, you can't be in here." Hanging out in the boys' locker room was bold, even for Zebby.

"Relax. No one else is in here. We need to talk, Amr."

"I need to get dressed." I shivered as I turned to unlock my locker. I took my clothes out and laid them on the bench next to Zebby, but she didn't make any move to leave.

I sighed. "Come on, Zeb. Go!"

"I know you're not milkandhoney," she said finally. "I checked the history of the site. The fable was up there that morning, just like you said it was."

Well, that was something, anyway. "So why didn't

you check the history right from the start if you didn't believe me?"

"I don't know." Zebby looked down at the floor. "I should have."

"Yeah, you should have." I pulled my shirt on, then sat down beside her. "I probably should have told you about that fable, too. I shouldn't have just taken it down without saying anything."

"Why did you?" Zebby asked.

"I don't know. I was going to tell you, but I forgot. I just got so tired of all that milkandhoney stuff. That's why I took it down. Don't you get tired of it?"

"Of course I get tired of it. But when you run a newspaper, you can't just take stuff down because you're tired of it."

"Are you sure? It's our newspaper; we can do whatever we want."

"It doesn't always feel like our newspaper," Zebby said, slouching down on the bench. "It feels like it's just this big gossip site about Lilly Clarke. How did that happen, Amr?"

I didn't have an answer.

"Did milkandhoney ever complain that you took the fable down?" Zebby asked. "Or did they ever try and put it back up?"

"No. I think they've been too busy getting their new site up and running. Did you see that 'We Hate Lilly Clarke' website?"

Zebby nodded. "That's when I knew you couldn't be milkandhoney. It's too mean."

"Yeah."

"Did you really think *I* was milkandhoney?" Zebby asked.

"I wondered," I said. "But I didn't really think so. Not until you thought *I* was. That made me really mad."

"I know. I'm sorry."

"Me, too."

 ## Zebby:

It was depressing how much of the Truth about Truman website was devoted to gossip about Lilly. That whole thing had sort of taken on a life of its own, and I wasn't sure what to do.

I always wanted the Truth about Truman to be a true and honest newspaper about middle school life. I wanted it to be something that everyone could relate to, and I wanted everyone to feel like it belonged to them, and they could post whatever they wanted without anyone telling them that what they were thinking or feeling wasn't okay.

And I guess in a sense, it was all that. People did feel comfortable posting whatever they wanted. I guess I had hoped that the stuff they posted would be a little more newsworthy than "Look! Lilly Clarke used to be fat." Or "Oh, no! Lilly Clarke might be gay!"

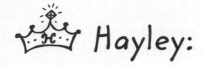 Hayley:

Lilly hadn't been in school all week. Which was really weird because Lilly never missed school.

"I wonder what's wrong with her," Cassie said during lunch.

"Maybe she's got some horrible, incurable disease," Kylie said as she bit into her apple.

"She *is* a horrible, incurable disease," Brianna muttered.

"Brianna!" I said, pretending to be shocked. "That's not very nice." But then I sort of smiled.

"Maybe she's not coming back," Cassie said.

"Maybe she's afraid to come back," Kylie said. "You know, because she doesn't have any friends."

"Aw, poor baby," I said. "I wouldn't like school if it wasn't for you guys, but I'd still come to school. I'd just find other friends."

"No kidding. What a loser," Brianna said.

"So, who wants to come over after school and help me judge the We Hate Lilly stories we've received so far?" I asked.

Brianna grinned. "I think we *all* want to help with that, Hayley," she said.

Everyone else nodded eagerly. Everyone except Kylie.

"What?" I asked her.

Kylie shrugged. "I was just thinking," she said, stirring her salad around on her plate. "That We Hate Lilly website is supposed to be totally anonymous, right? No one knows it's our website. And most people don't even know who any of those screen names are."

"So," I said, wondering what she was getting at.

"Well, how are we supposed to give someone a prize if we don't know who they are and they don't know who we are?"

Leave it to Kylie to obsess about something like that.

"We'll figure something out," Brianna said right away.

"Yeah," I echoed. "We can email the winner or something." Like Brianna said, we'd figure something out.

 ## Trevor:

I overheard Lilly's friends talking about her during lunch. Nice. With friends like them, who needs enemies?

I wondered if it ever occurred to any of those girls that sometimes kids who are bullied just snap. There have been all sorts of articles about this in the news and on TV.

Sara Murphy and me, we're used to being picked on, but Lilly's not. Frankly, I wondered if she could take all this abuse. What if she freaked out and…did something really bad?

Was anyone else worried about Lilly? I wondered. Any of the teachers? Mrs. Horton? Did any of them even have any clue what was going on? Probably not. Teachers and counselors were usually the last to know anything.

 Lilly:

I had a "slight recovery" over the weekend, but then got worse again on Monday. All in all, I missed three days of school. After three days, my mom may have figured out what was going on, because she wouldn't leave me alone with the thermometer in my mouth anymore. Which meant I couldn't hold it up against my light and make the silver stuff go up.

I tried to get her to go get me a drink of water, but she said to wait until after the thermometer was ready. And when it was ready, I suddenly had no fever.

"That's good news," Mom said, shaking the thermometer down. "You can go back to school."

"But I still don't feel good," I moaned, clutching my stomach. "I don't think I can go to school." *There was no way I could go to school!*

Mom came over and sat down on the bed next to me. "Tell me what's going on, Lilly," she said. "Why don't you want to go to school?"

"Because I don't feel good."

"It seems like there's something else going on. You like school. You like being with your friends—"

Yeah, back when I actually *had* friends, I thought.

"Are you having some sort of problem with your friends?" Mom asked.

"No," I grumbled. Because what I was having was more than "a problem." It was a catastrophe. My friends

118

didn't like me anymore. *Nobody* liked me.

"I just don't feel good," I said. "Please, Mom! Can't I just stay home for one more day?" I really, really needed to stay home for one more day. *At least* one more day.

Mom pressed her lips together and frowned. "Not unless you can give me a good reason for why you need to stay home."

"Isn't not feeling well a good enough reason?" I asked.

"Not after three days," Mom said. "Not when I'm not seeing any symptoms. You say your stomach hurts, but you're not throwing up and you're eating well. If anything, you're eating more than usual. I really don't think you're sick, honey. I think there's something else going on."

Even if I told her what was going on, she still probably wouldn't let me stay home. She'd tell me it would blow over, that my friends wouldn't stay mad forever. She wouldn't even get that they're not mad. There's a big difference between simply "being mad" and not liking someone anymore.

"Well, if you're not going to tell me what's going on, then you're going to have to go to school." Mom stood up and yanked the covers off of me.

I yelped.

"Come on. Get up." Mom went over to my dresser, opened my bottom drawer, pulled out a pair of jeans (even though I hardly ever wore plain old jeans anymore) and tossed them at me. She tossed me some socks and underwear, too. And finally a blouse from my closet.

A blouse that didn't even look good with jeans.

"I want you dressed and ready to go in fifteen minutes!" Mom said firmly. Then she walked out of my room and pulled my door closed behind her.

I swallowed hard, then raised myself up to a sitting position.

Well, fine, I thought, reaching for my clothes. She could make me get up and get dressed. She could even drive me to school. But once I was there, she couldn't make me stay.

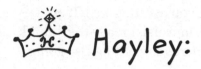 Hayley:

"Did you see what someone wrote on the We Hate Lilly page this morning?" Kylie asked in a low voice on the way to school on Wednesday.

"No. What?" Brianna asked, peering around her seat. Brianna and I had the middle seats in my mom's van. Kylie, Cassie, and Morgan sat behind us.

Kylie checked to make sure my mom couldn't hear us, then we all leaned our heads together and Kylie said in a low voice, "Someone made a list of 'the top ten things you'd like to see happen to Lilly Clarke.' There are things on there like 'fall down the stairs' and 'choke on her own vomit' and 'jump off a cliff.' "

Cassie giggled. "Oh, wow," she said. "I haven't read that yet."

"Me, either," Brianna said.

"You guys!" Kylie looked totally offended.

"What?" Cassie asked.

"Don't you find some of this just a little bit . . . disturbing? I mean, choking on her own vomit? Jumping off a cliff? She'd *die!*"

Everyone turned to me. Like they didn't know whether all this was disturbing or not.

I rolled my eyes. "You are so dramatic, Kylie!"

After all, *I* was the one who wrote the Top Ten Things You'd Like to See Happen to Lilly Clarke. But my friends didn't know that yet. I was going to tell them when they all agreed this was the piece that should win our We Hate Lilly contest. Wasn't Kylie the one who got all worked up about people finding out who we are when we had to give someone the five dollars? Well, fine. Let her figure out another solution then.

"It's not like whoever wrote that is planning to go over to Lilly's house and *kill* her or anything," Brianna told Kylie.

"Yeah, it's just stuff someone wrote on a website," Cassie added. "It doesn't mean anything."

"Right," Morgan nodded.

Kylie hugged her backpack to her chest. "I don't know," she said softly. "How would you feel if you read stuff like that about you on a website?"

I was getting a little tired of Kylie's attitude. "Why are you so worried about Lilly all of a sudden?" I blurted. "Do you actually *like* her again? Do you want to be her friend?"

"No," Kylie said, barely above a whisper.

"Good," I said. Because what happened to Lilly could easily happen to Kylie, too. I hoped she realized that.

 Lilly:

Mom kept trying to get me to talk on the way to school, but I just hugged my backpack to my chest and stared straight ahead out the front window.

"If you won't tell me what's wrong, how do you expect me to help you?" Mom asked.

I didn't expect her to help me.

"Please, Lilly. Talk to me."

I couldn't talk to her. I couldn't talk to anyone.

My eyes welled with tears when Mom pulled into the carpool line at school, but I bit down on my lip and blinked them back.

Mom tried one more time. "What *is* it, honey?" she asked.

I got out of the car and slammed the door behind me. I wanted to disappear. I wanted to go someplace where there were no people. And no computers. Someplace where I could be totally alone and no one would ever find me.

I could tell my mom was watching me walk toward the school. I could feel her eyes on my back. So I kept walking until I finally saw her pull away from the curb. But then, instead of heading for the front door, I turned and walked casually alongside the buses. When I was sure no one was looking, I darted around the corner of the school. I inched along the side of the building and rounded another corner to the back of the building.

I'd never been back here before. I heard pans rattling and water running. I was back by the kitchen.

I crept around a dumpster and just about tripped over a pair of legs. The legs belonged to Sara Murphy, who was sitting in the dirt, her back pressed against the dumpster, reading a computer gaming magazine.

Great. "What are *you* doing here?" I asked.

She looked up at me, but didn't say anything. Big surprise.

"Why am I always running into you?"

·Still nothing. No expression. Nothing.

"WHY DON'T YOU EVER SAY ANYTHING?!"

Why was I even talking to a girl who never talks back? I had to get out of there. I darted through the hedge that separated school property from the neighborhood. Then I ran and ran and ran, until I couldn't run anymore.

 **Sara:**

Everyone wants to know why I don't talk. I think it's hilarious when people come up to me and ask me to my face, "Hey, freak girl! Why don't you ever talk?" If they know I DON'T TALK, why do they ask me a question and expect to get an answer?

First of all, I *do* talk. I talk at home. I talk to my online friends. I just don't talk at school.

Why? Because I decided not to back in sixth grade. It all started when Lilly and those girls made fun of my eczema in gym every day. Yeah, my skin was kind of gross. It still is, I guess. But what am I supposed to say when people call me Fungus and they don't want to sit next to me and they don't want to touch me. It's not like I can make the eczema go away. So, I stopped saying anything. I couldn't control what the other kids said to me, but I *could* control what I said (or didn't say) back.

At first it was just those mean girls that I refused to talk to. But then I extended it to everyone. Even teachers. From the moment I stepped onto school property until the moment I left school property, I went silent. I didn't ask questions; I didn't answer questions. I didn't say a word. It was kind of empowering!

People get a little freaked out when you suddenly stop talking, though. I remember Mrs. Horton called me into her office and asked me what was wrong.

I didn't answer.

"Your teachers are concerned about you, Sara," she said. "There's got to be a reason you stopped speaking."

I just stared back at her. I didn't want to tell her the reason.

Mrs. Horton didn't know what to do with me, so she called my mother, and we all three had a conference. She told my mother I needed more help than the school could give me and that I should see a psychologist.

"My daughter doesn't need a psychologist," my mother said. I'm not sure my mother believes in psychologists. "Sara talks just fine at home. If she's not talking here at school, maybe it's because she has nothing to say."

All of a sudden, Mrs. Horton was the one who had nothing to say.

That was two years ago. By now most people have figured out that I DON'T TALK and they leave me alone. Which is way better than when they all picked on me. I much prefer being known as "the weird girl who doesn't talk" than "the weird girl with the disgusting skin problem."

You may not realize this, but people who don't talk all the time are usually better observers and better listeners. For instance, I know everything that goes on at this school. I even know who milkandhoney is. But I'll never tell. I'm that weird girl who doesn't talk, remember?

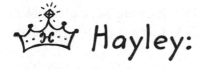 ## Hayley:

Lilly's mom called while I was doing my nails. "Have you seen Lilly today?" she asked.

I held the phone against my ear with my shoulder. "No," I said, as I painted my pinkie nail deep red. "I don't think she was in school, was she?" I knew perfectly well she wasn't in school.

"Well, I *thought* she was in school," Lilly's mom said. "But then the school secretary called me at work around ten o'clock this morning and told me Lilly wasn't in school. I thought it was a mistake. I dropped Lilly off myself, so I know she was there. But then she didn't call in after school like she's supposed to, and she didn't answer the phone when I called home. So I got worried and came home. She's not here, Hayley. Her backpack's not here, either, so she hasn't been home. Do you have any idea where she could be?"

I blew on my nails. "No, I'm sorry," I said. "I don't have any idea."

Lilly's mom sighed. "Is there something going on with her that I should know about?"

This was not something I wanted to get into with Lilly's mom. "What do you mean?" I asked vaguely.

"I don't know . . . have you noticed any change in her behavior lately? It doesn't seem like you girls have been getting together quite as much lately. Has she been hanging out with some other kids? Maybe kids she shouldn't be hanging out with? Kids who could be getting her into trouble?"

I bit the inside of my cheek. I wasn't quite sure what to say to that.

"I really don't know who she's hanging out with these days, Mrs. Clarke," I said.

"Are you sure? If you're trying to protect her, trying to keep her from getting into trouble—"

"I'm not," I insisted, anxious to get her off the phone. "It's just . . . like you said. Lilly hasn't really been hanging out with us much lately."

"Why not? Did you girls have a fight?"

I paused. "Not a fight, exactly . . . " How do you tell someone's mom that their daughter just isn't making the cut anymore?

"I'm making you uncomfortable," Lilly's mom said.

"Uh . . . yeah. Sort of."

"I don't mean to. I just want to know where Lilly is."

"Well, if I knew anything, Mrs. Clarke, I'd tell you. Really."

Lilly's mom sighed again. "Okay. Well, thanks, Hayley." And then she finally hung up.

Brianna:

I was freaking out! Lilly's *mom* called me. Apparently she'd called Hayley, too, but for some reason Hayley wasn't anywhere near as freaked out as I was.

"Did Lilly's mom tell you that Lilly's missing?" I shrieked into the phone. I'd called Hayley as soon as I hung up with Mrs. Clarke.

"She's not 'missing,'" Hayley said in a bored voice. "Lilly's mom just doesn't know where she is."

"Neither does anyone else," I said. "Did Lilly's mom ask you if there was anything going on between all of us, any reason we weren't all hanging out together anymore?"

"Yes, and I blew her off. Why? What did you tell her?"

"I didn't tell her anything," I said. Which was true. "But what about . . . did you tell her about . . . " I didn't quite know how to word it.

"Did I tell her about what?" Hayley asked impatiently.

"You know," I said, my heart pounding. "About our website?"

"Of course not," Hayley said. "Did you?"

"No. But what if she finds out about it? What if Lilly ran away or something because of our website?" If she did, we were going to be in major trouble.

"They can't prove that site is ours," Hayley said. "Our names aren't on there anywhere. Besides, what about those other sites—the Lilly's Lesbian Diary and the Truth about Truman? Those are just as bad as ours, and we didn't have anything to do with those."

I bit my lip. "Yeah, I guess," I said. But that didn't make me feel any less freaked out.

 **Zebby:**

The phone rang while I was doing my homework. It was Lilly's mom, of all people. She wanted to know whether I'd seen Lilly at all that day.

I just kind of "uh'ed" at her for a few seconds because I couldn't figure out why she was asking *me*. Finally, I had to just come right out and say, "You know, Mrs. Clarke, Lilly and I haven't exactly been friends for the last two years . . . "

"Yes, but even if you're not friends anymore, you still know each other. You live in the same neighborhood. You see each other now and then. I just want to know whether you saw her in school today. Or after school."

"I don't know," I said, trying to remember. "I don't think so." Honestly, I try to pay as little attention to Lilly as possible.

So then Mrs. Clarke started asking me a bunch of questions about whether I'd noticed anything strange about Lilly lately, whether she was still hanging around with the same girls, whether she had new friends, whether I had any idea why she might not have wanted to go to school. Each question she asked made me squirm just a little more because of course I knew why Lilly wouldn't want to go to school. So did everyone else at Truman.

Mrs. Clarke sounded so worried. So scared. She must have called like fifty other people before she called me. Had *no one* told her what was going on at school? Had no one told her her daughter was getting trashed online?

"You know, I'm sorry you and Amr and Lilly have all gone separate ways," Mrs. Clarke said. Her voice was all choky. "But if you don't know anything . . . "

"Wait!" I said, before Mrs. Clarke hung up. Because *somebody* had to tell her what was going on.

 Amr:

"You told Lilly's mom about the Truth about Truman?" I practically yelled into the phone. Why would she do that?

"I had to," Zebby said. "You should have heard her, Amr. She's really worried. She asked me if Lilly was having trouble with kids at school. What was I supposed to do? Tell her everything was fine?"

"Couldn't you have just told her about the Lilly's Lesbian Diary site and the We Hate Lilly site? Did you have to tell her about the Truth about Truman?" If my parents found out I ran a website where people gossiped and posted mean things about other people, they'd *kill* me. That was why I took that fable off our website.

"I didn't think I could tell her about those without at least mentioning ours," Zebby said. "If she stumbled across the Truth about Truman on her own, she'd wonder why I didn't mention it. Besides, there's no reason we should have to hide. We're not the ones who posted any of that stuff about Lilly."

"Yeah, maybe," I said. "So what did she say? Did she get online and look at any of those sites while you were talking to her?"

"No, she—" All of a sudden Zebby stopped talking.

"She what?" I asked.

Zebby didn't respond.

"Hello?" I said. Had Zebby left me hanging here? I could hear voices in the background, so I knew we were still connected, even if she had suddenly gone away.

"Yo! Zeb? Are you still there?"

"Yeah, I'm here. Amr, look outside. There are a bunch of police cars in front of Lilly's house!"

"What? There are?" I went to the window and yanked open the shade. Zebby was right. There were two police cars in Lilly's driveway and two more parked on the street in front of her house.

 Zebby:

There were already a lot of people standing around in front of Lilly's house when my parents and I headed down the street. Some were talking to the police, others were clustered around Lilly's mom or just standing around looking serious.

Amr and his parents had just come out of their house. Amr's dad was dressed in business clothes; his mom wore a blue hijab. "What is going on?" she asked my mom.

"I don't know," my mom replied. "Zebby says Lilly is missing."

"Missing!" Amr's mother cried.

Our parents approached Lilly's mom to see if there was anything they could do to help. Amr and I hung back at the edge of the crowd.

A woman came over to us and introduced herself as Detective Marsh. "Are you two friends of Lilly's?" she asked as she turned to a fresh page in her small notebook.

Amr and I glanced at each other. "Not really," I said.

"We know her," Amr put in. "But we don't hang around with her."

"I see," Detective Marsh said. "And what are your names?"

We told her and Detective Marsh stopped writing. She turned back a couple of pages in her notebook, read a little bit, frowned, then raised her head.

"You're the kids who run one of those websites," she said.

* * * *

As soon as my mom and I walked in our house, my mom said, "I want to see this website you and Amr created."

She made it sound like the Truth about Truman School was some worthless website and that it was somehow *our* fault, mine and Amr's, that people posted all those mean things about Lilly. Detective Marsh was the same way. She wanted to know when we started the site, why we started it, did we know what was on there, did we post any of those mean things about Lilly, did we know who did, did we think it was wise to set things up so that anyone could post whatever they wanted, and on and on and on.

"It's really not *that* bad," I told my mom as we sat down at my computer. My dad was out with a bunch of people searching for Lilly.

Mom folded her arms across her chest and waited for the site to come up.

"It's not like the whole purpose of our site is to trash Lilly. It's not. The Truth about Truman School is an online newspaper. It's a place where anyone at school can go to write about whatever is on their minds."

"Even if 'whatever is on their minds' is hurtful to someone else?" Mom asked.

"Well—" That wasn't my intention.

When the site came up, Mom reached for my mouse.

I watched her scroll past the "Who's the Biggest Poser at Our School" headline, Lilly's picture, and all the comments attached to it. She clicked on the link to Lilly's Lesbian Diary and read through everything on there. Then she went back to our site and clicked on the link to the We Hate Lilly website. With every click of the mouse, the line of her jaw seemed to tighten.

When she finished reading, she blinked about ten times. Which meant she was upset. "What in the world makes you think it's okay to post things like this on a website?" she asked.

"I didn't post any of that stuff about Lilly. I posted the article about the Lego robotics team, and the article about school food, and the article about—"

"But you let other people post it," she interrupted.

I clucked my tongue. "I can't control what other people post!"

"Sure you can. It's *your* website. If you and Amr don't control what people post on it, who does?"

"Nobody," I said, sitting up a little straighter. "That's the point. It's a freedom of speech issue. We say right on the front page that we aren't going to censor anyone. So what can we do? We can't go back on our word."

Mom cocked her head, like *you know better than that, Zebby.*

"It's not like I *wanted* anyone to post this stuff," I went on. "In fact, I would have preferred they not post it since it's not exactly news."

"So take it down," Mom said simply.

"It's not that simple—"

"It is *exactly* that simple, Zebby. You're the editor of this website. That means you're the one who decides what's fit for publication. Do you really think *this*," she pointed at the link to Lilly's Lesbian Diary, "is something worthy of publication?"

I lowered my eyes. "Not exactly—"

"Then take it down. In fact, while you're at it, I'd like you to take down *all* the articles, drawings, photographs, polls, and comments that could somehow be considered hurtful or offensive to someone else."

"There wouldn't be much left if I did that," I muttered.

"Then take the whole thing down," Mom said.

"WHAT?" I leaped to my feet in protest.

Mom stood up, too. "You heard me. You either need to find a way to run this website responsibly, or you need to take it down."

 Amr:

It was really quiet at our house the next morning. The explosion had come the night before, when my mom made me show her the Truth about Truman. She got really mad when she saw the site and she said I had to take it down. I told her I couldn't do that without talking to Zebby.

"Then talk to Zebby," she said.

But I never saw Zebby online last night. So our site was still up.

Now this morning, my mom stood by the kitchen sink, sipping a cup of tea. She hadn't made any breakfast. When she saw me coming, she poured a bowl of Cheerios and set it in front of me, but I didn't feel like eating it.

My dad was still upstairs getting ready for work. He and a bunch of other people from our neighborhood had been out late searching for Lilly the night before, but they never found her.

My stomach was all twisted up. I couldn't eat, so I got up and dumped my cereal down the sink. "I better go," I said, even though I really didn't need to leave for school for another ten minutes yet.

"Have you talked to Zebby?" Mom asked just before I went out the door.

"Not yet," I admitted.

"Today, Amr. You talk to her today and then you take that website down."

"Okay," I said. I knew Zebby's mom was worried about our site, too. They went back to their house about the same time my mom and I came back here. But Zebby's folks aren't as strict as mine are. I couldn't imagine they expected her to take the whole site down. How was I supposed to tell Zebby that that was what my mom wanted me to do?

I needed time. Time to figure out the exact right way to bring it up. So I decided not to pick her up on my way to school. I went the other way around the block. Past Lilly's house.

There was still a police car parked in front of Lilly's house. Just one, though. I wondered if this was the same one that was parked there the night before, or if this was a different one that had come this morning. There was another car I didn't recognize in the driveway, too. An unmarked police car, maybe?

While I was staring at their house, the front door opened and Lilly's mom stepped outside with a police officer and some other man who looked a little bit familiar, but I wasn't sure who he was at first. He was tall and thin, and he dressed like a guy who worked in an office and made a lot of money. They were so busy talking they didn't pay any attention to me as I walked past their house. Two houses later it hit me. I knew who that guy was. Lilly's *dad*.

 Zebby:

Amr forgot to stop and pick me up on his way to school that day. And I was so busy thinking about our website that I lost track of time and had to run all the way to school. I made it, though. With about thirty seconds to spare.

My mom said I had to find a way to run the Truth about Truman School responsibly or take the whole thing down. I still wasn't sure what she meant by "run it responsibly." Did she really expect me to look at every single comment on the site and decide whether it was okay to leave up or whether it had to come down? How was I supposed to decide what was okay and what wasn't? Where did you draw the line?

A lot of people knew Lilly was missing now. I don't know where they found out about it; I never posted anything about it on the site. But there were a lot of where's-Lilly posts and a lot of talk about did-she-go-willingly-or-did-something-bad-happen-to-her that morning? *I* wondered if something bad had happened to her.

There was one question nobody was asking, though: why did Lilly take off in the first place? Did anyone else wonder if maybe it was our fault she took off? All of us who either wrote mean things about her online or who read the things other people wrote and didn't do anything about it. Or was it *my* fault because I'm the one who started the Truth About Truman? And I'm the one who let people post whatever they wanted.

 Anonymous:

I never expected things to go so far. I never expected other kids to join in like they did. And I certainly never expected Lilly to disappear.

Wherever she was, she was okay, wasn't she? I mean, we would've heard something if she wasn't, right?

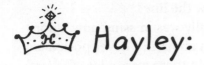 Hayley:

It was all over school. Lilly Clarke never came home last night. A lot of people came up to us that morning to see if we knew where she was or what had happened to her. But how would we know? We haven't been hanging out with her.

"So, what's the deal?" Morgan asked during lunch. "Did she run away?"

"Did she run away because of the We Hate Lilly website?" Kylie asked.

"If she did, she must really be messed up," I said as I opened my yogurt.

"What do you mean?" Kylie asked.

"Well, anyone that would run away just because of a website has to be unstable," I said.

Brianna and Cassie agreed.

Personally, I thought Lilly Clarke was getting entirely too much attention. She probably loved the idea that everyone was all worried about her. Wherever she was, I was sure she was fine.

 Zebby:

Lilly wasn't the type to just take off somewhere on her own. I couldn't imagine her sleeping outside in a box like a homeless person. I couldn't imagine her hopping on some random bus to who-knows-where. So where *was* she? I wondered during lunch.

"Hey, Zeb," Amr said, interrupting my thoughts. "We need to talk."

"Okay," I said, glancing over at him.

He stirred his macaroni and cheese around on his plate. "My mom says we have to take the Truth about Truman down," he mumbled.

"My mom said basically the same thing."

Amr's head popped up. "She did?"

"Well, she said we have to take all the mean stuff off our website or we have to take the whole site down," I corrected.

"What?" Trevor Pearson cried from the next table over. "You can't take the Truth about Truman down!"

"Why not?" What did he care whether we took the site down or not? A lot of people had given him a hard time about that comic strip he posted, and some kids even grabbed a comic he was working on in class and wrecked it.

"Because it's real," Trevor replied. "Because it's the truth. It's the only place where everyone at school can say whatever they want."

"That was the idea," I said, shoving my tray away. "But things didn't work out quite like I expected. Sometimes when you let people say whatever they want, they say things that aren't very nice."

"Duh," Trevor said. "This is middle school. I still think you should keep the site up."

"Why?"

"Because it tells the truth," Trevor said. "And the truth is, middle school sucks!"

Yeah, it did. Sometimes.

That was the whole reason I started the Truth about Truman to begin with. I wanted to give everyone a voice. Even the people who thought middle school sucked.

Was it even possible to publish a newspaper or website that really was for everyone . . . without upsetting anyone?

Brianna:

We had a test in math that day. I had already answered all the questions I could (which wasn't many), so I kept watching the clock. Fifteen more minutes until class got out.

Bzzz! Bzzz! Mr. Wesack's phone rang.

A lot of people shifted in their seats as Mr. Wesack got up to answer his phone. "Hello? Yes?" Mr. Wesack glanced over at me, so I quickly lowered my eyes to my test.

"I'll send her right down," Mr. Wesack said, hanging up the phone. "Brianna?"

My head popped up. "Huh?"

"Mr. Gates would like to see you in his office."

I felt a stab of fear in the pit of my stomach. "Why?" I choked. Why would Mr. Gates want to see *me*?

"I'm sure you'll find out when you get there," Mr. Wesack said.

Heart pounding, I stood up and started for the door. "Take your things," Mr. Wesack said. Which was even more unnerving. "I don't think you'll be back before the end of the period."

I went back to my desk and gathered up all my stuff.

Kylie mouthed at me, "Why do you have to go to the office?"

I had no idea.

I gave my half-filled-out test to Mr. Wesack, then headed down to the office. The secretary, Mrs. White, had a grim look on her face when I walked in. "They're waiting for you in Mr. Gates's office, Brianna," she said. "You can go on in."

"Okay." I didn't even know Mrs. White knew my name.

Mr. Gates's door was open, so I slowly made my way toward it. I froze in the doorway. *My parents were in there!* My mom, my dad, and my stepdad. All three of them were sitting around a table with Mr. Gates . . . and *two police officers.*

What was going on?

Mr. Gates stood up when he saw me. "Have a seat, Brianna," he said, closing the door behind me.

I swallowed, then took a seat in the only chair available. Right between Mr. Gates and the lady police officer. Everyone was staring at me.

There was a laptop computer on the table in front of Mr. Gates. He turned it so I could see the screen. "Does this look familiar to you, Brianna?" The We Hate Lilly Clarke website was up on the screen.

I swallowed again, but didn't say anything. My heart was really pounding now.

"Did you make that website, Brianna?" my mom asked.

I was too scared to answer.

"Did you?" my mom asked again when I didn't answer.

I did . . . but I didn't do it by myself. Hayley, Cassie, Kylie, and Morgan helped. In fact, they probably did more of it than I did. But I couldn't say that. Not in front of the police. *Why were the police here?*

"With the help of your Internet service provider, we were able to trace the IP address of this website to your home, Brianna," the tall, skinny officer explained.

"Is there anybody else in your home who could have set this website up?" the lady officer asked.

I slumped down in my chair. *Oh, boy. I was in big trouble!*

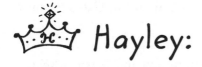 Hayley:

Kylie told us that Brianna got called to the office during math.

"Why?" I asked.

Kylie didn't know. So we made a detour past the office on our way to sixth period. We didn't see Brianna in there, but we saw something else. There was a police car parked in front of our school.

"Why is there a police car at our school?" Cassie asked.

"I don't know," I said. But I didn't like it. There was a police car at our school and Brianna got called to the office. Were those two things somehow related?

Morgan grabbed my arm. "Do you think they know about the We Hate Lilly website?" she cried.

"SHH!" I glared at her, nodding toward the office. What if they had a speaker or something in there that made it possible for them to hear what people were saying out in the hallway?

Mrs. White was the only person in the main office and she didn't *act* like she heard us. She was busy typing something at the computer.

"Even if they do know about it, the only way they'd know any of us had anything to do with it is if one of us told someone," I said.

"Well, I sure didn't tell anyone," Morgan said.

"Neither did I," Cassie said.

"It's possible they traced that website back to the computer it was created on," Kylie said, not looking at me.

"Can they *do* that?" Cassie cried.

"Maybe," I said. "But even if they did, why would anyone call the police over it?" Sure, it wasn't very nice to hate someone, but was it really a *crime*? What was the big deal?

Cassie chewed her bottom lip. "What if Brianna tells that we all worked on it?" she asked.

"She won't," I said with more confidence than I actually felt. We don't like rats in our group, and Brianna knows it.

But Brianna is weak. And I wasn't sure where her breaking point was.

Brianna:

"Are you sure those other girls you hang out with had nothing to do with this?" my mom asked. "The website says '*We* Hate Lilly Clarke.'"

"It was just me," I mumbled. Because I don't rat on my friends! But it seemed a little unfair that I was the only one who was going to get in trouble for this.

"So 'milkandhoney' is just one person," the lady police officer said.

What? Wait a minute. "I never said I was milkandhoney," I told the lady police officer.

The two police officers looked confused. "You just admitted you created the We Hate Lilly website," the tall, skinny officer said.

"Yeah, but that doesn't mean I'm milkandhoney. I'm *not* milkandhoney!"

Mr. Gates typed something on his laptop, then turned it around so I could see it. He had the Truth About Truman website up. "There's a link to the We Hate Lilly Clarke website on this other website. And that link was posted by milkandhoney."

Uh-oh. I had forgotten about that. "I uh, borrowed the name milkandhoney. I'm not milkandhoney," I said, knowing it sounded lame. But it was the truth! Milkandhoney had posted all this other stuff about Lilly, so we decided we'd post our link to the We Hate Lilly Clarke website under that name, too. It was Hayley's idea. She said that way nobody would know it was our website. Because obviously *we* weren't milkandhoney.

"Who did you borrow the name from?" the lady police officer asked.

"From . . . this other person who was posting all this stuff about Lilly. Hey, if you traced that post back to my house, can't you trace milkandhoney's other posts?" I asked. Now, I was thinking! "Then you'd know milkandhoney wasn't me."

It turned out they already had traced milkandhoney's other posts. To the school media center computers. The police had dates and times. All after school.

"Mrs. Conway gave us a list of kids who have been in the media center after school," Mr. Gates said. "Your name was on that list, Brianna."

I slumped down in my chair. Of course my name was on it. Hayley, Lilly, and I stayed after school and looked up cheerleading stuff in the media center.

"W-what about those other websites?" I sputtered. "Did you find the people who created the Lilly's Lesbian Diary website or the Truth about Truman website. Maybe they're milkandhoney?"

"We've spoken with the students who created the Truth about Truman," the lady police officer said. "And while no one has claimed credit for Lilly's Lesbian Diary, we were able to trace that one back to the school computers, too."

They all stared at me like they were waiting for something.

What were they waiting for? I wondered.

Then I got it. They thought *I* did Lilly's Lesbian Diary, too.

❓ Anonymous:

I expected more. More from the school, I mean. I figured if they ever found out what was going on, they'd confiscate all the computers, round up every single person who ever posted anything bad about Lilly online, call in extra counselors, and have a big school assembly to talk about cyberbullying, maybe even bullying in general. But none of that happened.

When they called Brianna Brinkman to the office, I was sure they'd be calling my name next. If they knew about Brianna, they had to know about me.

But apparently, they didn't.

Before the day was over, everyone knew that Brianna had been suspended for writing mean things about Lilly Clarke online and for creating the We Hate Lilly website and the Lilly's Lesbian Diary site, too, and that she was milkandhoney. People thought Brianna was responsible for pretty much everything bad people posted about Lilly.

Obviously, people were wrong.

You might be wondering whether I felt bad about Brianna getting suspended while I pretty much got away with everything I did. Not really. Because I couldn't feel too bad about Brianna Brinkman getting in trouble.

 Zebby:

So Brianna Brinkman got suspended. I *knew* milkandhoney would turn out to be one of the popular kids.

But just because milkandhoney got caught didn't mean the whole thing was over. I still had to figure out what to do about our website. *Find a responsible way to run it or take the whole thing down.* My mom said I was grounded until I did one or the other.

And Lilly was still missing.

I have to tell you, I never meant for things to get so out of control. I just wanted to publish an alternative newspaper. I wanted to publish good, hard-hitting articles that said something about the middle-school experience. I wanted to publish something that *mattered.*

But the Truth about Truman School didn't matter to anyone except me and Amr. The only reason anybody read it was to see who said what about someone else.

That was never what I had in mind.

So in the end, I took the whole thing down. I replaced everything with just one line on the main page: The Truth about Truman School is . . . <click here>.

If you clicked, another page came up that said, "people there can be really mean."

 Amr:

I couldn't concentrate on my homework that night. My dad joined the search for Lilly again after work. I guess there had been people searching pretty much round the clock.

Where could she have gone? It was hard to picture her wandering around out in the woods somewhere. Or sleeping outside. Lilly was not the sleep-outside type.

Maybe she was hiding in Wal-Mart or something? Hadn't I read a story in the news a while back about somebody living in a Wal-Mart? But if she was, wouldn't someone have seen her and recognized her? This wasn't that big a town.

She wouldn't have done something stupid like hitch-hiked her way out of here, would she? Like back before anyone even knew she was missing? What if she ended up in a car with some psycho who—I didn't want to think about it.

No she wouldn't have hitchhiked, I decided. She had to be hiding out somewhere around here. Somewhere where no one would see her.

I wondered where *I* would go if I wanted to hide from everyone for a while? Probably to that old tree house we used to play in in the woods. It wasn't too likely *Lilly* would go there, though. Like I said, she wasn't exactly the outdoor type. Plus she didn't even like the tree house. She used to make fun of me and Zebby for still wanting to play in it when we were in sixth grade.

But the more I thought about it, the more I wondered, what if she *was* up there? Had anyone even checked?

 ## Zebby:

Amr called me while I was getting ready for bed that night. He wondered if Lilly was hiding out in our old tree house.

"Oh, I doubt it," I said. I don't think she ever liked the tree house as much as Amr and I did. Even when we were all friends.

"Yeah, you're probably right," Amr said.

But what if she *was* up there? All those people were out looking for her . . . what if she really was that close?

"I'll see you tomorrow," Amr said.

"Wait!" I cried before he hung up. "Maybe we should go up there and check things out?"

"By ourselves?"

"Sure," I said. "It won't take very long, and she's probably not there anyway."

"Okay. I'll meet you in your backyard in about ten minutes," Amr said.

I pulled a pair of sweatpants over my pajama bottoms and grabbed my gray jacket.

"I need to go outside and talk to Amr for a minute," I told my mom as I strolled past the family room.

My mom looked up from the cross-stitch she was

doing. "Now? It's pretty late, Zebby. Can't you talk to him on the phone?"

"No, he's on his way over. It won't take long. We'll just be out back." I walked away before she could make me stay inside.

I grabbed a flashlight from the utility room and went out the back door. Amr was already waiting by my old swing set. He looked a little nervous.

"Are you ready?" he asked, turning his flashlight on.

"Yeah," I said. Then we plunged into the dark, dark woods behind my house. We had to walk single file because of all the bushes and trees. Leaves and twigs crackled beneath our feet. Even with the flashlights, we could hardly see anything.

We came to the rickety little bridge that went over the creek and I stopped.

"Why are you stopping?" Amr asked.

I shined my flashlight down at the bridge. "We're not little kids anymore," I said. "Do you think this bridge will still hold us?"

Amr looked at it. "It will if we cross separately," he decided. Then to prove it, he hurried across. No problem. When he got to the other side, he turned around and shined his flashlight back on the bridge. "Your turn," he said.

Gingerly, I took one . . . two . . . three . . . four steps on my tiptoes and then I was standing next to Amr. The woods weren't as thick on this side of the creek, so we could walk side by side.

All of a sudden, Amr stopped. He turned his

flashlight off and told me to turn mine off, too.

"What? Why?"

"Just turn it off." Amr grabbed the flashlight out of my hand and turned it off himself. Now it was pitch black.

I could feel Amr standing perfectly still beside me. Watching. Listening.

"What?" I said again, still not seeing or hearing what he was.

"I saw a light," Amr said in a low voice.

"Where?" I squinted, then opened my eyes wide, but I had no idea how he could see anything out here without a flashlight.

"Up ahead. Around the tree house."

I grabbed onto Amr's sleeve and we slowly made our way through the trees. I knew the tree house was in one of those old oak trees at the edge of the woods, right before you got to the grassy field. There were pieces of wood nailed into the trunk for steps. And an actual wooden tree house loomed in the large branches of the tree. It had a door, windows, even a roof. No one knew for sure who built it, but it was probably the guy who owned the land where all our houses are now. People said there used to be a big farmhouse right where my house is.

Amr, Lilly, and I had spent hours up in that tree house when we were little. But I hadn't been there in at least two years. I wasn't even sure I could find the right tree in the dark. But Amr seemed to know exactly where we were going. I followed him as he forged a

trail through the thick underbrush. When we reached
the edge of the woods, light from a half moon lit up the
grassy field in front of us. Amr steered us to the right
and we walked along the edge of the woods a little
further.

"There it is," Amr said, stopping in front of a tree
with wood boards nailed to the trunk.

I couldn't believe he found it in the dark.

I peered up at the dark blob.

"Do you really think she's up there?" I asked.

Amr shrugged. "There's only one way to find out."
He held his flashlight under his arm, put his foot on the
bottom rung, and started climbing.

 Amr:

I sure hoped Lilly was in the tree house. If my mom
found out I snuck out of the house and went wandering
around the woods after dark with a girl, even if that girl
was Zebby, she would not be happy. Unless Zebby and I
actually found Lilly.

I climbed up onto the platform, and with the flashlight held tight against my side, I crawled over to the
door. I reached for the knob and turned. It didn't budge.
"I think it's locked," I told Zebby.

"Don't you remember?" she said as she carefully
made her way over to me. "The knob sticks. You have to
pull up at the same time you're turning."

Zebby reached around me and opened the door. We crawled into the little house and turned on our flashlights at the exact same time.

"Ouch!" Something hard whacked me in the forehead. I dropped my flashlight and it rolled along the wood floor.

"Oh, my gosh!" Zebby said, stunned. "You really are up here!"

I rubbed my forehead and Zebby aimed her flashlight at a girl who looked like a sad imitation of Lilly, huddled in the corner. The girl wore jeans and a torn blouse, and her hair hung in tangled clumps around her blotchy face. She didn't look anything like the Lilly I knew. She had obviously been crying. A lot.

She shrunk back a little and put her arm up over her eyes to block the light. "GET OUT!" she yelled at us.

I felt something go whizzing by me. It hit the wall behind me with a thump. I grabbed my flashlight and aimed it behind me so I could see what else had almost hit me. A dirty white tennis shoe. And there was another one just like it beside me.

"YOU HAVE NO RIGHT TO BE HERE!" Lilly screamed, squinting in the bright light.

"What do you mean we have no right to be here?" Zebby yelled back, still shining her flashlight in Lilly's face. "This isn't your private tree house. We've probably spent way more time up here than you have."

Lilly's face crumpled and she started crying again. Wailing, really. I don't think I've ever heard anyone cry like that.

Zebby lowered her flashlight. I could tell by the look

on her face that she felt bad for making Lilly cry again. She motioned for me to do something, but I didn't know what to do. So I motioned for her to do something. But she didn't know what to do, either. So we just sat there and waited for Lilly to cry herself out.

 ## Lilly:

What made Zebby and Amr, of all people, decide to come looking for me? And what made them decide to look for me in the tree house? I could tell by all the cobwebs and bugs I found up here that no one else had been up here in a very long time. That's why this seemed like the perfect hiding place.

I knew I had until after school before my mom would realize I was gone yesterday. So when I left school, I went home and quickly gathered up all the stuff I thought I'd need: sleeping bag, pillow, flashlight, extra clothes, food, water, book of Sudoku puzzles. It took me five trips to get everything up into the tree house, but then I was set.

A couple of people actually climbed up here last night. I think one of the people was Zebby's dad. But they couldn't get the door open. I crouched down under the window and sat really still when they shined their flashlights in. They didn't see me, so eventually they left.

I thought that was it. I could stay up here forever now. They wouldn't come looking for me up here again.

The only problem was I couldn't go home to use the bathroom or have a shower or get more stuff because my mom was always there. I ended up using the woods for a bathroom (gross!). And I was starting to run out of food and water. I didn't know how long I could really stay.

"Everyone's looking for you," Zebby said after a little while.

"So?" I sniffed. My head ached and I needed a tissue, but I didn't have any up here.

"So, you've been gone a long time. Maybe you should come down now?" Amr said.

"I'm not ever going down," I said.

"You can't stay up here forever," Zebby said.

I glared at her. "Why not?"

"Because you don't have enough food," Zebby said. She shined her flashlight in all my grocery bags, as though it was any of her business how much food I had. "And you don't have a bathroom. And, well...*we're* not staying up here forever. So when we go down, we'll just tell everyone you're up here anyway."

"You better not!" I warned.

"We will," Zebby said. And I knew they would. Why wouldn't they?

But they didn't make any move to leave, and neither did I. We just sat in silence for a few minutes.

Then Amr said out of the blue, "Brianna got suspended."

"She did?" This was news. "How come?"

"Because she's the one who posted all that stuff about you online," Amr said. "She's milkandhoney."

Funny, I used to think Brianna was milkandhoney, too. But I'd had plenty of time to think while I was up in the tree house a day and a half. I shook my head. "I don't think Brianna's milkandhoney."

"Yes, she is," Zebby said. "The police traced an IP address back to her."

I still didn't believe it. "Maybe somebody set things up so it looked like she was milkandhoney," I said.

"Who would do something like that?" Zebby asked.

"Maybe . . . the two of you?" Milkandhoney *had* to be Zebby and Amr. There was no one else it could be.

Zebby let out a big breath of air. "For the thousandth time, Amr and I are NOT milkandhoney!"

"Well, it's not Brianna," I said. "She never had a copy of that awful picture of me."

"It was in the memory book," Amr said. "All she needed was for someone to give her a copy of the memory book. Anyone from Hoover could have done that."

"Anyone who saved it for three years," I said. How many people really hung onto their memory books from elementary school? Zebby probably did; Zebby hung onto everything.

"None of my friends even knew I used to be fat," I went on. "They didn't know it was me in that picture. Not until you guys announced it." Zebby opened her mouth to object, but I talked right over her. "It has to be someone from Hoover; no one else from Hoover hates me as much as you guys; therefore, milkandhoney has to be you!"

"Trust me, Lilly," Amr said. "Zebby and I aren't

milkandhoney. So if you don't think Brianna is, either, then let's see if we can figure out who *is*." He shifted position. "Here's what we know so far: Milkandhoney is obviously somebody who doesn't like you, or somebody who has a grudge against you for some reason. It's *probably* somebody who went to Hoover, but not necessarily..."

That sounded like Zebby and Amr to me . . .

"Milkandhoney is a coward," Zebby said. "We know that, too."

I raised my eyebrow. "You're calling yourself a coward now? That's big of you."

"Anyone who says nasty things online under an anonymous screen name has to be a coward," she said.

"It's got to be someone who knows something about computers," Amr said. "They scanned that picture in and uploaded it themselves. They knew how to send stuff anonymously and set up a fake email address. They knew something about webpage design. That We Hate Lilly website was pretty crude, but the other one, Lilly's Lesbian Diary, that one had animations and stuff. Someone knew what they were doing when they created that."

"It's also got to be somebody who hangs out in the media center after school since that's where a lot of the messages originated," Zebby said.

"Who hangs out in the media center after school?" Amr asked.

"Once again, *you* guys," I said.

"Not me," Amr said. "I have to go home and pray every day after school."

"You and your friends were in there quite a bit these

157

last couple of weeks," Zebby said to me.

"Not that much," I said. "Just when we were looking up cheerleading stuff."

"Brianna and Hayley were in there by themselves a couple times this past week," Zebby said. "And Trevor Pearson and Sara Murphy are in there almost every day."

My blood went cold.

Why hadn't I figured this out before?

"I think I know who milkandhoney is," I said.

 **Zebby:**

"Who?" I asked. "Who's milkandhoney?"

But Lilly wouldn't tell me. She just all of a sudden headed for the door. Which surprised me a little. How did figuring out who milkandhoney was suddenly make her decide to come down from the tree house?

I stuck my flashlight in my pocket. "What are you going to do?" I asked as I scrambled down the ladder behind her. Amr put his flashlight in his mouth and followed after me.

"Are you going to confront milkandhoney?" I called down to Lilly. "Are you going to tell the police? Or Mr. Gates?"

"I don't know," Lilly said when we were both on solid ground again. "For now, I'm just going to go home. If that's okay with you."

I raised my hands in surrender. "Fine. Whatever." I never said anything about Lilly made sense.

We tromped through the woods in silence, our flashlights lighting the way. As soon as we stepped into my backyard, we found out half the neighborhood was now out looking for Amr and me.

Our parents weren't too mad when they found us, though. Not when they saw we'd brought Lilly back with us.

 **Lilly:**

I had a long talk with my parents when I got back. I found out they knew about those websites and what people were saying about me online. They also knew that all my friends had dumped me. And I was actually glad they knew; that way I didn't have to explain it to them.

What they didn't know was how much of a struggle the last three years had been for me. Even when I had friends. I was always so afraid I was going to do something wrong, or gain weight again, and they wouldn't want to be friends with me anymore.

I never told anyone this, but I didn't always like who I was when I was with those girls. There were times I didn't even recognize myself. I was…mean sometimes. And I said or did things just to impress everyone else. I was so worried about what they thought about everything that I never stopped to ask myself, *what do I think about this?*

Maybe it was time to figure out what I thought about a few things.

I told my parents I didn't want to back to Truman anymore. I wanted to go to Roosevelt, the other middle school. Or even St. Jude's. Even though I'm not Catholic. I didn't care where I went as long as I didn't have to go back to Truman.

"That's ridiculous!" my dad said. "Those kids who have been bothering you have been caught and punished. There's no reason you can't go back to school!"

Brianna was the only one who'd been caught. And I found out later that even though she wasn't milkand-honey, she was the one who started the We Hate Lilly website. She and my other so-called friends. But that didn't matter. Believe it or not, I didn't want to switch schools just because everyone at Truman hated me. I wanted to switch schools because I needed a fresh start. I needed to figure out who I was…away from my old Hoover friends and my Truman friends and everyone who's ever known me.

My dad didn't buy it. "If we let you switch schools, we'd just be allowing you to run away," he said. "You can't run away from your problems, Lilly."

"It's not running away!" I argued. "How come it's okay for adults to get new jobs and move away and even get divorced when they want out of something? But it's not okay when kids need a fresh start?"

Neither of my parents had an answer to that.

"Let's talk about this in the morning," my mom said. Then she sent me to bed.

I had a hard time falling asleep. I could hear my parents talking in the other room, but I couldn't hear what they were saying. Finally, around midnight, I heard the front door open and close and I heard a car start up and pull out of the driveway. My dad was going home.

My mom let me sleep in the next morning. She didn't make me go to school. But she did ask if I still wanted to change schools.

I told her I did, so she made some phone calls. Half an hour later it was all set. I would be starting Roosevelt on Monday.

Okay, maybe my dad was right. Maybe I was running away. But sometimes running away was an okay choice.

 Zebby:

So that's it. It's all over. Lilly's back, but I guess she's not coming back to Truman. I can't say I blame her. The language arts teachers took a break from our regularly scheduled curriculum to talk to us about cyberbullying.

I took notes: Technology has made it possible for kids to harass each other in new ways. What is cyberbullying? It's when you bully someone online. Why is it bad? Because you don't see the person you're bullying and they don't see you. So you say things you might not say otherwise.

Once I realized we weren't going to be tested on this, I stopped taking notes.

Mrs. Michael said someone had been hurt by the Truth about Truman and those other websites. She didn't name names, but we all knew who she was talking about.

And now the whole school was supposed to write about what happened with the Truth about Truman and those other sites, how the whole thing got so out of control, how it affected us, and how we felt about it. She said it wasn't just one person who was responsible; our whole school was responsible.

I got what she was saying, but I couldn't help but feel I was a little more responsible than everyone else. My feelings were all jumbled up inside. I still didn't like Lilly all that much, but we had a history together. And I felt bad about what happened. I didn't write any of that mean stuff about her, but I created a website that made it possible for other people to write stuff about her. It almost made me wish there had never been a Truth about Truman website.

 Trevor:

I feel like a little kid who's being made to write one hundred times, "I will not cyberbully anyone." What good is that going to do? Do the teachers really think that by making us write a paper about it no one's ever going to go online and say something mean about someone else ever again? They're fooling themselves if that's what they think!

Mrs. Michael said, "Because you can be anonymous online, the person you show the world online is usually not the real you." I think she's dead wrong about that. I think the person you show online is exactly the person you really are. The person you show in real life is the one that's fake. Think about it. Most people are chameleons. They act different around different people. What's real about that?

Mrs. Michael is probably one of those do-gooders who sees all the bad stuff people say or do online and then thinks, "That's not real." But the truth is, that's the only thing that *is* real. The person you are when no one's looking, or when no one else knows who you are . . . that's the person you really are!

 Amr:

I got a little annoyed by how the teachers made such a big deal about this *cyber*bullying thing. Like cyber-bullying was somehow worse than any other kind of bullying. Bullying is bullying. Whether it's being done on the computer or anywhere else.

A lot of adults are blaming the whole thing on computers. I have news for them. Kids have been bullying each other a lot longer than computers have been around. So don't blame computers. Blame the kids!

Brianna:

Besides being suspended for five days, my mom and stepdad grounded me for a whole month. Plus they took the computer out of my room. They said I didn't deserve to have a computer in my room since I had shown them I didn't know how to use one responsibly. From now on, when I want to use the computer, I have to use it in the family room, where I get, like, no privacy.

My mom even made me write Lilly a letter of apology, which she *read* to make sure it was good enough. Didn't anyone realize we were just goofing around? It wasn't any big deal.

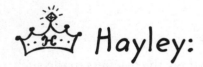

Hayley:

Okay. We got it. Saying bad things about someone online, whether it's on a website, in an email or an instant message, or a text message is bad, bad, bad. We're bad kids. We go to a bad school. We'll never do it again.

Can we move on now?

 ## Lilly:

I still had some unfinished business before I started at Roosevelt. Call me crazy, but I wanted to meet with milkandhoney in person.

Anonymous:

I got an email from Lilly! It said: *Dear milkandhoney, I know who you are.* Obviously she did know who I was since the email came directly to me. *I don't want to get you in trouble. I just want to talk to you. I think I know why you did this. I think we should talk in person rather than in email. Meet me at the monkey bars at our old school at 4:00. If you show up, I promise I won't tell anyone about you. But if you DON'T show up, I MIGHT tell.*

I didn't get it. Why would Lilly want to talk to me in person? And why wouldn't she want to get me in trouble? Why wouldn't she want me to pay for my role in all this? I certainly wanted her to pay for everything she ever did to me and every other unpopular kid at Truman.

Trevor:

Lilly was perched on top of the monkey bars when I arrived at Hoover that day. She watched me walk across the playground. There were some elementary school kids playing basketball, and a couple more over by the swings. But Lilly and I were the only kids hanging around the monkey bars.

I squinted up at her. "How did you know it was me?"

Her eyes were focused on something just over my head. "I didn't," she said. "I *thought* it was you, but I didn't know for sure until right this second."

"Oh," I said, digging my toe into the sand. "Are you going to tell on me now? Now that you know it's me?"

"I said I wouldn't." She still wasn't looking directly at me.

"Well, then why did you want me to meet you?"

Now, she looked at me. "I wanted to say I was sorry, Trevor."

I blinked. "Y-you wanted to say you were sorry?" There was nothing she could have said that would have surprised me more. "For what?"

"For what I said about you. And your mom. You know. Two years ago. Right before she died."

Oh.

"I assume that's why you did this."

You're so ugly your mom would probably keel over and die of embarrassment for giving birth to you. That was what she'd said to me.

"It was a horrible thing to say," Lilly said in a small voice. "Especially when . . . you know . . . your mom . . . "

"Died?" I filled in.

Lilly nodded, then looked away.

I leaned back against the bar. I didn't know what to say. I wanted to bring Lilly Clarke down. I wanted to make her feel as bad as she made other people feel. And . . . it looked like I had. But it didn't bring me as much satisfaction as I thought it would.

Remember when I said I thought the person you show the world online is the person you really are? If that's true, then I'm a bully. I'm no better than Lilly or Reece or Jonathan or any of the other kids who have bullied me all these years.

At first I thought I could just stay Anonymous forever. But in the end, I decided I had to write the whole truth. I also apologized to Lilly. Maybe now I can finally move on.

 Zebby:

I couldn't believe who was instant messaging me. Lilly! "can i talk to u?" she typed.

"u r already talking to me," I typed back.

"right. i saw u took the Truth about Truman down."

"yeah." I had taken the whole thing down that morning. Even the "kids at Truman are mean" message. There didn't seem to be much point in leaving it up.

"thanks."

"you're welcome. but i didn't take it down for u. i took it down because it wasn't what I wanted it to be."

"what did you want it to be?"

I doubted Lilly would understand. But I told her anyway. "i wanted it to be something that mattered. something where every1 could write about their own middle-school experience. but instead it turned into a gossip website where people talked about everyone else rather than themselves."

"maybe u could still do something with it that matters?"

"like what?"

"i don't know. maybe it could be a place where people can go to talk about bullying?"

Hmm.

I had to admit, that was an interesting idea. A *very* interesting idea. Even if it did come from Lilly.

I called Amr and he liked the idea as much as I did. He was the one who thought we should start by putting up the story of what happened to Lilly and then have a forum where anyone anywhere in the world (not just kids from Truman) can write in and talk about bullying.

We don't want to approve every message that gets posted, but we'll keep an eye on things. If people start posting nasty things or if they try and turn this into another gossip site, we'll delete those messages. As site owners (and editors!), we've decided it's okay to do that.

Maybe in the end, the Truth about Truman.com will mean something after all.

Once Amr and I worked all this out, I called Lilly. Don't get the idea we were suddenly friends again. We weren't. It's just . . . it only seemed right to call her. Since she gave me the idea and all. "Hey, do you want to help with this new website?" I asked.

She paused for a second. "Really? You want me to help?"

"Sure. It was your idea."

"Yeah, I guess it was." I could almost hear her smiling over the phone. "Okay. Hey, maybe I'll meet some kids at Roosevelt who would want to help, too."

"That'd be great," I said. "We want this site to really be for everyone."

So that's it. That's our story. I couldn't get a lot of kids to write about what happened. Big surprise. Some kids will *tell* you anything you want to know, but when it comes to writing . . . especially something they don't have to write, well, most kids won't do it. I was really surprised Hayley and Brianna were willing to write about it. Sometimes the popular kids will surprise you.

I don't know if our story will help anyone or not, but it's there. For better or worse.

—Zebby Bower, over and out.

The Truth About Truman School
General Discussion Guide

1. What did you think of the book? Did you like it? Why or why not? Do you think it was realistic? Why or why not?

2. Which character did you like best? Which character did you like least? Why?

3. Choose two of the main characters in the book. How are they alike? How are they different?

4. Do you think the teachers at Truman School knew what was going on?

5. Why do you think things got so out of control on truthabouttruman.com?

6. Do you think Zebby regretted starting her website? Was starting it a mistake?

7. Do you think Zebby felt bad about what happened to Lilly? What about Amr? Hayley? Brianna? Kylie? Trevor? Reece? Sara?

8. Have you ever wanted to drop a friend the way Lilly wanted to drop Zebby and Amr in sixth grade? Why? How did you do it?

9. If you were going to start a website, what would you put on it? Would you let other people post to it? If so, would you set it up so that you had to approve other people's posts or would you let

people post whatever they wanted? Under what circumstances would you remove someone else's post?

10. Do you think milkandhoney had a good reason for doing what he/she did to Lilly?

11. Were you surprised to find out who milkandhoney was or was that the person you thought it was all along? What clues led you to believe it was this person? What clues led you to believe it was someone else?

12. Do you think it's a good idea for Lilly to go to a new school? What do you think life is going to be like for her there?

13. Why do you think the author ended the book the way she did? Why did the author "punish" or "not punish" each character the way she did? Would you have written a different ending? Why or why not?

14. Have you ever bullied anyone online? Have you ever been bullied online? Have you ever seen someone else be bullied online?

15. Have your views on cyberbullying changed since you've read this book? How?

Cyberbullying
Discussion Guide

1. Do you think cyberbullying is a serious problem or do you think it's no big deal?

2. Do you think the media make cyberbullying look worse than it actually is?

3. Do you think people have the right to say whatever they want about others on the Internet? Explain.

4. Do you think people present themselves differently online than they do in person? How? Why would a person want to act differently online than they would in person?

5. Have you ever bullied anyone online? Why did you do it?

6. Have you ever been bullied online? Did you tell anyone it was happening? What did you do?

7. Why do you think kids are reluctant to tell anyone if they're being bullied online?

8. Have you ever watched a friend of yours bully someone else online? Did you say anything about it to your friend? Why or why not? And if you did, what happened?

9. Do you think cyberbullying is worse than any other kind of bullying? Why or why not?

10. Why do you think people bully others online? Do you think people who bully others online are the same people who bully on the playground? Explain.

11. When does a "joke" become an example of cyberbullying?

12. Do you think schools should get involved in cyberbullying incidents? Why or why not?

13. Do you think cyberbullying will be a bigger problem ten years from now or do you think it will be a smaller problem? Why do you feel that way? What about twenty-five years from now? What about fifty years from now?

14. What can we do about cyberbullying? How can we prevent it? How do we stop it once it's occurred?

Cyberbullying
Resources

What should you do if you're being bullied online?
1. Don't respond. Any response may fuel the fire.

2. Try and identify the bully. Even if he or she is using a fake name, help may be available through a website moderator or your Internet Service provider.

3. Block communication with the bully if you can.

4. Consider saving the messages and/or images as evidence.

5. Tell a friend, parent, teacher, police officer or other adult you trust.

Online Safety Tips:
1. Don't post your full name, address, phone number, school name, parents' names, social security number online.

2. Don't say anything online that you wouldn't say to someone's face.

3. Don't post anything online that you wouldn't want your grandma to see.

4. Don't share your passwords with anyone other than your parents.

5. Don't meet someone face-to-face if you only know them online.

6. Talk to your parents about what you do online.

Resources

http://www.cyberbullying.us/resources.php
The Cyberbullying Research Center is dedicated to
providing up-to-date information about the nature,
extent, causes, and consequences of cyberbullying.

http://www.ncpc.org/topics/cyberbullying
The National Crime Prevention Council's mission is
to help people keep themselves, their families, and their
communities safe from crime.

http://www.stopcyberbullying.org
and **http://www.wiredsafety.com**
WiredSafety.org is the largest and oldest online safety,
education, and help group in the world.

About Dori Hillestad Butler

Dori Hillestad Butler is the author of more than 30 books for children, including picture books, chapter books and middle grade novels. Her middle grade novels *Sliding Into Home; Trading Places with Tank Talbott; Do You Know the Monkey Man* and *The Truth About Truman School* have been on children's choice award lists in sixteen different states. She's been a ghostwriter for several popular series, including the *Sweet Valley Twins* and *The Boxcar Children*.

Her Edgar® Award-winning series *The Buddy Files* is a chapter book series about a school therapy dog who solves mysteries. Dori and her dog, Mouse, are a registered pet partner team in Coralville, Iowa, where they participate in a program that promotes reading with dogs.

She grew up in southern Minnesota and now lives in Coralville, IA with her husband, son, dog and cat.

You may also enjoy the following books from author David Patneaude...

Colder Than Ice
HC   978-0-8075-8135-3 • $15.99
PB   978-0-8075-8136-0 • $6.95
Age Levels: 9-12, Grades: 4-7

Sasquatch Reading Award Master List
Sunshine State Young Reader's Award Master List

Deadly Drive
PB   978-0-8075-0845-9 • $6.95
Age Levels: 11-14, Grades: 6-8

Mark Twain Award preliminary list

Framed in Fire
PB   978-0-8075-9096-6 • $5.95
Age Levels: 11-14, Grades: 6-9

SSLI Honor Book - Language Arts - 7-12 Novels
Golden Sower Award Master List – YA
Mark Twain Award Master List
Kentucky Bluegrass Award Master List - grades 6-8

Haunting at Home Plate
HC   978-0-8075-3181-5 $15.99
PB   978-0-8075-3182-2 $6.95
Age Levels: 9-13, Grades: 4-8

Texas Lone Star Master List
Volunteer State Book Award Intermediate Master List
West Virginia Children's Book Award Master List
Garden State Children's Book Award Master List
Sasquatch Reading Award Master List
Pennsylvania Young Reader's Choice Awards Master List
Sunshine State Young Reader's Award Master List
Young Hoosier Book Award Master List (Middle Grades)

The Last Man's Reward
HC   978-0-8075-4370-2 • $15.99
PB   978-0-8075-4371-9 • $5.95
Age Levels: 11-14, Grades: 5-8

Books for the Teen Age, New York Public Library
Sasquatch Reading Award Master List
Utah Children's Book Award Master List
Iowa Children's Choice Awards Master List
Volunteer State Book Award Master List
Rebecca Caudill Young Readers' Book Award Master List

A Piece of the Sky
HC   978-0-8075-6536-0 • $15.99
Age Levels: 10-13, Grades: 5-8

"This exciting treasure hunt has all the elements of a thriller, and the gun-wielding bad guy on the trail of the friends rocks the plot into hyper-mode. An entertaining light summer read."—*Kirkus Reviews*

Someone Was Watching
PB 978-0-8075-7532-1 • $6.95
Age Levels: 11-14, Grades: 6-9

Nebraska Golden Sower Young Adult Award Runner-Up
South Dakota Prairie Pasque Award
Texas Lone Star Reading List
Sunshine State Young Reader's Award Master List
Utah Children's Book Award
Young Hoosier Book Award Master List
Best of the Texas Lone Star Reading Lists
Runner-up for Rebecca Caudill Award